# STAR TREK®

# STAR FLEET

# TECHNICAL MANUAL

### FEDERATION CLASSIFIED

THIS MANUAL IS FOR THE SPECIFIC USE OF STAR FLEET
ACADEMY CADETS AND CONTAINS SELECTED MATERIAL
FROM THE DATA BANKS OF THE MASTER COMPUTER. UNDER
THE LAWS OF THE UNITED FEDERATION OF PLANETS AND
ITS MEMBER PLANETS UNAUTHORIZED USE, OR REPRODUC-
TION, IN WHOLE OR IN PART, OF THESE TECHNICAL ORDERS
OR ANY SUBSEQUENTLY ISSUED, WITHOUT THE WRITTEN
PERMISSION OF STAR FLEET OR ITS PLANETARY AGENTS IS
STRICTLY PROHIBITED.

## TRAINING COMMAND
## STAR FLEET ACADEMY

OFFICIAL VERSION FOR CADETS FROM
UNITED NATIONS, EARTH, SOL SYSTEM

## BALLANTINE BOOKS • NEW YORK

RESEARCHED AND COMPILED BY:
# FRANZ JOSEPH*
UNITED FEDERATION REPRESENTATIVE
MILITARY STAFF COMMITTEE
STAR FLEET HEADQUARTERS, 0 MARK 0, R5PC

WITH GRATEFUL APPRECIATION TO THESE CIVILIANS OF UNITED NATIONS/EARTH/SOL SYSTEM:

ANNE ANDERSON, JUDY LYNN DEL REY, FRED C. DURANT, III, IRVING FEINBERG, WALTER M. JEFFRIES, ROBERT H. JUSTMAN, IGOR LABONOFF, LOU MINDLING, GENE RODDENBERRY, WILLIAM THEISS, BJO TRIMBLE, & STEPHEN E. WHITFIELD

AND ESPECIALLY TO THESE CIVILIANS AND CIVILIAN AUXILIARIES:

ART CANFIL, DAVID BARBER, SHARON FERRARO, JAMIE HANRAHAN, DENNIS HUNT, TONI LAY, ROD MARCH, JEFF MAYNARD, ROBERT MROZ, SANDY SARRIS, KAREN LINDA SCHNAUBELT, JANICE SCOTT, GREG WEIR, CHARLES WEISS, HELEN YOUNG, MEMORY ALPHA, SPACE-TIME CONTINUUM, S.T.A.R. SAN DIEGO, STAR TREK ARCHIVES, & STAR TREK WELCOMMITTEE

PRINTINGS:
1ST EDITION STARDATE 7511.01
20TH ANNIVERSARY EDITION STARDATE 8609.01

21  22  23  24  25  26  27  28  29  30

THE PUBLISHER GRATEFULLY ACKNOWLEDGES THE COOPERATION OF PARAMOUNT TELEVISION, A DIVISION OF PARAMOUNT PICTURES CORPORATION, THE PRODUCERS OF THE STAR TREK TELEVISION SERIES, IN GRANTING PERMISSION TO PUBLISH THIS VOLUME.

*UNITED NATIONS/EARTH IDENTITY:
FRANZ JOSEPH DESIGNS

# FOREWORD I

PHOTOCOPY

## UNITED STATES MILITARY·FORCES
### GENERAL STAFF HEADQUARTERS
#### WASHINGTON, D.C, U.S.A.

memorandum to:   Franz Joseph Designs

from:            Col. Robert Argon, Director
                 Security Control/MFHQ

date:            15 April 1973

subject:         MF Security Docket #075140

enclosure:       one (1) copy of subject docket

1. Pursuant to your inquiry we are enclosing one (1) copy of subject
   docket without restrictions. The security classification has been
removed, and there is no longer any official interest in the matter.

2. The printed 'message' was: "ALERT.....ALERT.....UNITED FEDERATION
   FLEET HEADQUARTERS MASTER LIBRARY COMPUTER.....TO.....LIBRARY COMPUTER
.....ALL FEDERATION STARSHIPS ON SPECIAL SERVICE.....STARDATE 3113.....
SUBJECT.....TRANSMISSION OF UPDATED TECHNICAL MANUAL MASTER DATA SECTIONS
.....00:00:00.....00:00.00                              ...0:02
.....BEGIN TRANSMISSION....."

3. The message and the 'data sheets' which followed were found in the
   memory banks of the master computer at Security Control, Omaha MFB,
and were accidentally discovered in 1970 during a print-out run, while the
computer was being interrogated for another reason. A top security lid
was immediately clamped on the matter while an investigation was launched
to attempt to identify the source of the unusual transmission. Neither
the message or the data could be traced to any known country, or alliance,
in the World. All of the terminology, uniforms, weaponry, and other
material was completely foriegn to the terminology, uniforms, weaponry,
and other material known to be in existence at that time.

4. The investigation was terminated with a final determination that the
   whole affair had been a hoax. That the 'unusual' material had been
inserted into the computer as a prank. And the file was closed, while a
search was initiated to find the person, or persons, responsible for this
breach of Security Control. To date this effort has been fruitless.

# FOREWORD II

PHOTOCOPY

OFFICIAL USE ONLY
O MARK O R5PC

## STAR FLEET COMMAND
### STAR FLEET HEADQUARTERS
## UNITED FEDERATION OF PLANETS

SIDRE AEL SARDELAS, DIRECTOR
MILITARY STAFF COMMITTEE

STARDATE 3150.10

to:  All Divisions concerned
     Star Fleet Command

1.  Pursuant to the matter of the unauthorized transmission of SFAF
material (viz: SFHQ/Mastercom Computer Data) into the Master Computer at
Security Control, Omaha MFB, Earth, Sol System as of stardate 3113, the
Special Review Board examined the following pertinent documentation:

   (a) report of Capt. James T. Kirk, commanding, U.S.S. Enterprise;
   (b) report of Lt. Cmdr. Spock, First Officer, U.S.S. Enterprise;
   (c) report of the investigation by the Special Review Commission;
   (d) report of the historical events sequential review of the data
       banks of Mastercom/SFHQ;

2.  The Special Review Board has now concluded its determination.  It
finds: (1) that both Capt. James T. Kirk and Lt. Cmdr. Spock cannot be
faulted for the matter since it occurred in the routine computer-to-
computer transmission, which operates independently of the SFAF Communications Systems or human supervision; and: (2) that it occurred as the
result of an unpredicted, and unforeseen gravitational space-warp which
is now known to be a natural phenomenon within the galaxy; and (3) that
it was a purely random matter which occurred without human intervention
and therefore is considered to be a natural accidental occurrence in the
sequential train of historical events.

3.  The Special Review Board further finds that in the event the material
now stored in the data banks of the Master Computer at Security Control,
Omaha MFB, should become known in that time period, it would be advisable
to review whatever material is included in that storage to: (a) delete
any technology which is not known to Earth's technology in that time
period, in order to preserve the Prime Directive's doctrine of non-inter-
vention; and: (b) to correct any material which is determined to be "safe"
but which was distorted in the transmission.

4.  Therefore, the Planetary Relations Division of Star Fleet Command is
hereby assigned the task of this final determination in the event it should
become necessary, and all Divisions shall support this effort as required.
The Planetary Relations Division shall also prepare a final report upon
the conclusion of any actions they may take, for submission to the Federation Council.

## GENERAL INDEX

GENERAL INDEX

Note:   (*) indicates Manual Division and Section Title Page

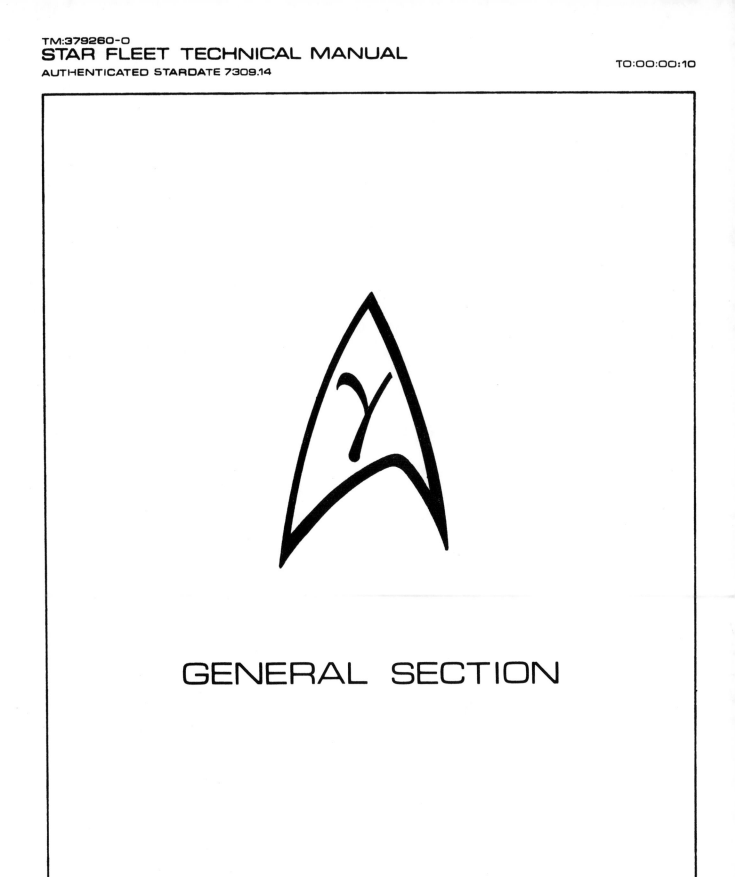

# GENERAL SECTION

## SECTION INDEX

| TO. NO: | SUBJECT: | CURRENT | REPLACES |
|---|---|---|---|
| 00:00:10 | GENERAL SECTION FLYSHEET | 7309.14 | |
| » » :12 | FOREWORD | * | |
| » » :14 | SECTION INDEX | 7407.29 | |
| » :01:00 | ARTICLES OF FEDERATION - DECL, CH. I, AR.1, P. 1, 2, & 3 | 7305.29 | |
| » » :01 | A.O.F. - CH. I, AR.1, P. 4, AR. 2, P.1,2,3,4, 5,6, & 7, CH. II, AR. 3, AR. 4, P.1 | » | |
| » » :02 | A.O.F. - CH. II, AR. 6, TO CH. IV, AR. 11, P. 3 | » | |
| » » :03 | A.O.F. - CH. IV, AR. 11, P. 4 TO AR. 17, P. 2 | » | |
| » » :04 | A.O.F. - CH. IV, AR. 17, P. 3 TO CH. V, AR. 23, P.1 | » | |
| » » :05 | A.O.F. - CH. V, AR. 23, P. 2 TO AR. 28, P.1 | » | |
| » » :06 | A.O.F. - CH. V, AR. 28, P. 3 TO CH. VI, AR. 35, P. 3 | » | |
| » » :07 | A.O.F. - CH. VI, AR. 36, P.1, TO CH. VII. AR. 43 | » | |
| » » :08 | A.O.F. - CH. VII, AR. 44 TO AR. 50 | » | |
| » » :09 | A.O.F. - CH. VII, AR. 51 TO CH. VIII, AR. 54, P. 1 | » | |
| » » :10 | A.O.F. - CH. VIII, AR. 54, P. 2 TO CH. IX, AR. 60 | » | |
| » » :11 | A.O.F. - CH. X, AR. 61 TO AR. 66, P.1 | » | |
| » » :12 | A.O.F. - CH. X, AR. 66, P. 2, TO CH. XI, AR. 73 | » | |
| » » :13 | A.O.F. - CH. XI, AR. 73 TO CH. XII, AR. 76 | » | |
| » » :14 | A.O.F. - CH. XII, AR. 77, P.1 TO AR. 83, P.1 | » | |
| » » :15 | A.O.F. - CH. XII, AR. 83, P. 2 TO CH. XIII AR. 87 | » | |
| » » :16 | A.O.F. - CH. XIII, AR. 88 TO CH. XIV, AR. 95 | » | |
| » » :17 | A.O.F. - CH. XIV, AR. 96 TO CH. XV, AR.101 | » | |
| » » :18 | A.O.F. - CH. XVI, AR. 102 TO CH. XVII, AR. 107 | » | |
| » » :19 | ARTICLES OF FEDERATION - CH. XVII, AR. 108 TO - FINAL | 7305.29 | |
| 00:01:20 | STATUTE - INTERPLANETARY SUPREME COURT OF JUSTICE | * | |
| » » :21 | » - CH. I, AR. 5, P. 3 TO AR. 7, P. 6 | * | |
| » » :22 | » - CH. I, AR. 7, P. 7 TO AR.11 | * | |
| » » :23 | » - CH. II, AR. 12 TO CH. II, AR. 14 | * | |
| » » :24 | » - CH. II, AR. 15 TO CH. III, AR.19, P. 3 | * | |
| » » :25 | » - CH III, AR. 19, P. 3 TO AR. 23, P.1 | * | |
| » » :26 | » - CH. III, AR. 23, P. 2 TO CH. V, AR. 27 | * | |
| » » :27 | STATUTE - CH V, AR. 28 TO - FINAL | * | |
| | | | |
| 00:01:30 | STATUTE REGULATING INTERPLANETARY COMMERCE | * | |
| » » :31 | » - PART I, SECT. 1, ITEM 12 TO 23 | * | |
| » » :32 | » - SECT. 2 TO PART II, SECT. 5, ITEM 01 | * | |
| » » :33 | » - SECT. 5, ITEM 02 TO SECT 6, ITEM 04 | * | |
| » » :34 | » - SECT. 6, ITEM 05 TO PART III, SECT. 10, ITEM 04 | * | |
| » » :35 | » - SECT. 11 TO PART IV, SECT. 16, ITEM 01 | * | |
| » » :36 | » - SECT. 16, ITEM 02 TO SECT. 17, ITEM 02 | * | |
| » » :37 | » - SECT. 18, ITEM 01 TO 07 | * | |
| » » :38 | » - SECT. 18, ITEM 08 TO PART V, SECT. 19, ITEM 05 | * | |
| » » :39 | » - SECT. 19, ITEM 06 TO SECT. 21 | * | |
| » » :40 | » - SECT. 21, ITEM 01 TO SECT. 22, ITEM 05 | * | |
| » » :41 | » - SECT. 23 TO SECT. 27, ITEM 01 | * | |
| » » :42 | » - SECT. 27, ITEM 02 TO SECT. 29, ITEM 04 | * | |
| » » :43 | » - SECT. 30 TO PART VI, SECT. 33, ITEM 01 | * | |
| » » :44 | › - SECT. 33, ITEM 02 TO PART VII, SECT. 36 | * | |
| » » :45 | » - SECT. 36, ITEM 01 TO SECT. 38, ITEM 01 | * | |
| » » :46 | » - SECT. 38, ITEM 02 TO SECT. 39, ITEM 03 | * | |
| » » :47 | » - SECT. 39, ITEM 04 TO SECT. 42 | * | |
| » » :48 | » - SECT. 43 TO SECT. 45 | * | |
| » » :49 | » - SECT. 46 TO PART VIII, SECT. 47, ITEM 02 | * | |
| » » :50 | » - SECT. 47, ITEM 03 TO SECT. 49, ITEM 02 | * | |

NOTE (*): NO CURRENT PRINT-OUT FROM MASTERCOM DATABANKS / SFHQ

## SECTION INDEX

| TO. NO: | SUBJECT: | CURRENT | REPLACES |
|---|---|---|---|
| 00:00:15 | SECTION INDEX | 7407.29 | |
| 00:01:51 | STATUTE-SECT. 49, ITEM 03 TO PART IX, SECT. 51, ITEM 05 | * | |
| » » :52 | » -SECT. 51, ITEM 06, TO PART X, SECT. 54 | * | |
| » » :53 | » -SECT. 55, ITEM 01 TO 05 | * | |
| » » :54 | » -SECT. 56 TO SECT. 57, ITEM 01 | * | |
| » » :55 | » -SECT. 57, ITEM 02 TO SECT. 58, ITEM 04 | * | |
| » » :56 | » -SECT. 58, ITEM 05 TO PART XI, SECT. 63 | * | |
| » » :57 | STATUTE-SECT 64 TO FINAL | * | |
| | | | |
| 00:01:60 | ROMULAN TREATY OF PEACE | 7305.30 | |
| » » :62 | ORGANIAN TREATY OF PEACE | 7305.30 | |
| | | | |
| 00:02:00 | UNITED FEDERATION OF PLANETS - BANNER | 7405.05 | |
| » » :01 | » » » » - SEAL | 7306.18 | |
| » » :02 | UNITED NATIONS, PLANET EARTH, SOL SYSTEM - FLAG | 7405.30 | |
| » » :03 | » » » » » » - SEAL | 7406.15 | |
| » » :04 | PLANETARY CONFEDERATION OF 40 ERIDANI - BANNER | 7407.13 | |
| » » :05 | » » » » - SIGNAT | 7407.09 | |
| » » :06 | UNITED PLANETS OF 61 CYGNI - SHIELD | 7407.06 | |
| » » :07 | » » » » - ARMS | 7407.07 | |
| » » :08 | STAR EMPIRE OF EPSILON INDII - STANDARD | 7407.05 | |
| » » :09 | » » » » » - SEAL | 7407.05 | |
| » » :10 | ALPHA CENTAURI CONCORDIUM OF PLANETS - PENNANT | 7406.24 | |
| » » :11 | » » » » - ARMS | 7406.25 | |
| 00:10:10 | UNIFORM COLOR CODE - STAR FLEET SPECIFICATION | 7407.04 | |
| » :10:00 | OFFICIAL TYPE STYLE - EARTH, SOL SYSTEM - SF SPEC. | 7405.10 | |
| » » :01 | » » » -ALPHA KENTAURUS - » » | 7407.05 | |

NOTE (*): NO CURRENT PRINT-OUT FROM MASTERCOM DATABANKS/SFHQ

# ARTICLES OF FEDERATION

WE THE INTELLIGENT LIFE-FORMS OF THE
UNITED FEDERATION OF PLANETS DETERMINED

TO SAVE SUCCEEDING GENERATIONS FROM THE SCOURGE OF INTRA-GALACTIC WAR
WHICH HAS BROUGHT UNTOLD HORROR AND SUFFERING TO OUR PLANETARY SOCIAL
SYSTEMS, AND

TO REAFFIRM FAITH IN THE FUNDAMENTAL INTELLIGENT LIFE-FORM RIGHTS, IN
THE DIGNITY AND WORTH OF THE INTELLIGENT LIFE-FORM PERSON, TO THE EQUAL
RIGHTS OF MALE AND FEMALE AND OF PLANETARY SOCIAL SYSTEMS LARGE AND
SMALL, AND

TO ESTABLISH CONDITIONS UNDER WHICH JUSTICE AND MUTUAL RESPECT FOR THE
OBLIGATIONS ARISING FROM TREATIES AND OTHER SOURCES OF INTERPLANETARY
LAW CAN BE MAINTAINED, AND

TO PROMOTE SOCIAL PROGRESS AND BETTER STANDARDS OF LIFE IN LARGER
FREEDOM,

AND TO THESE ENDS

TO PRACTISE BENEVOLENT TOLERANCE AND LIVE TOGETHER IN PEACE WITH ONE
ANOTHER AS GOOD NEIGHBORS, AND

TO UNITE OUR STRENGTH TO MAINTAIN INTRA-GALACTIC PEACE AND SECURITY,
AND

TO ENSURE BY THE ACCEPTANCE OF PRINCIPLES AND THE INSTITUTION OF METHODS
THAT ARMED FORCE SHALL NOT BE USED EXCEPT IN THE COMMON DEFENSE, AND

TO EMPLOY INTRA-GALACTIC MACHINERY FOR THE PROMOTION OF THE ECONOMIC
AND SOCIAL ADVANCEMENT OF ALL INTELLIGENT LIFE-FORMS,

HAVE RESOLVED TO COMBINE OUR EFFORTS
TO ACCOMPLISH THESE AIMS.

ACCORDINGLY, THE RESPECTIVE SOCIAL SYSTEMS, THROUGH REPRESENTATIVES
ASSEMBLED ON THE PLANET BABEL, WHO HAVE EXHIBITED THEIR FULL POWERS TO
BE IN GOOD AND DUE FORM, HAVE AGREED TO THESE ARTICLES OF FEDERATION OF
THE UNITED FEDERATION OF PLANETS, AND DO HEREBY ESTABLISH AN INTER-
PLANETARY ORGANIZATION TO BE KNOWN AS THE UNITED FEDERATION OF PLANETS.

## CHAPTER I
### PURPOSES AND PRINCIPLES

#### ARTICLE 1

THE PURPOSES OF THE UNITED FEDERATION OF PLANETS ARE:

1.  TO MAINTAIN INTERPLANETARY PEACE AND SECURITY WITHIN THE TREATY EXPLORA-
TION TERRITORY, AND TO THAT END:  TO TAKE EFFECTIVE COLLECTIVE MEASURES FOR
THE PREVENTION OF THREATS TO THE PEACE, THE SUPPRESSION OF ACTS OF AGGRES-
SION, AND TO BRING ABOUT BY PEACEFUL MEANS, AND EMPLOYING THE PRINCIPLES OF
JUSTICE AND INTRA-GALACTIC LAW, ADJUSTMENT OR SETTLEMENT OF INTERPLANETARY
DISPUTES WHICH MIGHT LEAD TO A BREACH OF THE PEACE;

2.  TO DEVELOP FRIENDLY RELATIONS AMONG PLANETS BASED ON RESPECT FOR THE
PRINCIPLES OF EQUAL RIGHTS AND SELF-DETERMINATION OF INTELLIGENT LIFE-FORMS,
AND TO OTHER APPROPRIATE MEASURES TO STRENGTHEN UNIVERSAL PEACE;

3.  TO ACHIEVE INTERPLANETARY COOPERATION IN SOLVING INTRA-GALACTIC PROBLEMS
OF ECONOMIC, SOCIAL, CULTURAL, OR HUMANITARIAN CHARACTER; IN PROMOTING AND
ENCOURAGING RESPECT FOR INTELLIGENT LIFE-FORM RIGHTS; AND FOR FUNDAMENTAL
FREEDOMS FOR ALL WITHOUT DISTINCTION AS TO CULTURE, SEX, LIFE-FORM, OR
RELIGOUS BELIEF; AND

ARTICLES OF FEDERATION

4.  TO BE A CENTER FOR CONCILIENCE OF THE ACTIONS OF ALL SOCIAL SYSTEMS IN THE ATTAINMENT OF THESE COMMON ENDS.

ARTICLE 2

THE FEDERATION AND ITS MEMBERS, IN PURSUIT OF THE PURPOSES STATED, SHALL ACT IN ACCORDANCE WITH THE FOLLOWING PRINCIPLES:

1.  THE FEDERATION IS BASED ON THE SOVERIEGN EQUALITY OF ALL ITS MEMBERS;

2.  IN ORDER TO ENSURE TO ALL OF THEM THE RIGHTS AND BENEFITS RESULTING FROM MEMBERSHIP, ALL MEMBERS SHALL FULFILL IN GOOD FAITH THE OBLIGATIONS ASSUMED BY THEM IN ACCORDANCE WITH THESE ARTICLES OF FEDERATION;

3.  ALL MEMBERS SHALL SETTLE THEIR INTERPLANETARY DISPUTES BY PEACEFUL MEANS IN SUCH MANNER THAT INTRA-GALACTIC PEACE, SECURITY, AND JUSTICE, ARE NOT ENDANGERED;

4.  IN ALL INTERPLANETARY RELATIONS, ALL MEMBERS SHALL REFRAIN FROM THE THREAT, OR USE, OF FORCE AGAINST THE TERRITORIAL INTEGRITY OR POLITICAL INDEPENDENCE OF ANY PLANETARY SOCIAL SYSTEM, OR IN ANY MANNER INCONSISTENT WITH THE PURPOSES OF THE UNITED FEDERATION;

5.  ALL MEMBERS SHALL GIVE THE UNITED FEDERATION EVERY ASSISTANCE IN ANY ACTION TAKEN IN ACCORDANCE WITH THESE ARTICLES OF FEDERATION, AND SHALL RE-FRAIN FROM ASSISTING ANY PLANETARY SOCIAL SYSTEM AGAINST WHICH THE FEDERATION IS TAKING PREVENTIVE OR ENFORCEMENT ACTION;

6.  THE UNITED FEDERATION SHALL ENSURE THAT PLANETARY SOCIAL SYSTEMS WHICH ARE NOT MEMBERS OF THE FEDERATION ACT IN ACCORDANCE WITH THESE PRINCIPLES AS NECESSARY FOR THE MAINTENANCE OF INTRA-GALACTIC PEACE AND SECURITY;

7.  NOTHING WITHIN THESE ARTICLES OF FEDERATION SHALL AUTHORIZE THE FEDERA-TION TO INTERVENE IN MATTERS WHICH ARE ESSENTIALLY THE DOMESTIC JURISDIC-TION OF ANY PLANETARY SOCIAL SYSTEM, OR SHALL REQUIRE THE MEMBERS TO SUBMIT SUCH MATTERS TO SETTLEMENT UNDER THESE ARTICLES OF FEDERATION; BUT THIS PRINCIPLE SHALL NOT PREJUDICE THE APPLICATION OF ENFORCEMENT MEASURES UNDER CHAPTER VII.

## CHAPTER II
MEMBERSHIP

ARTICLE 3

THE ORIGINAL MEMBERS OF THE UNITED FEDERATION OF PLANETS SHALL BE THOSE PLANETARY SOCIAL SYSTEMS WHICH, HAVING PARTICIPATED IN THE INTERPLANETARY CONFERENCE ON INTERPLANETARY FEDERATION AT BABEL, OR HAVING PREVIOUSLY SIGNED THE DECLARATION OF THE UNITED FEDERATION OF PLANETS OF STARDATE 0963, SIGN THESE ARTICLES OF FEDERATION AND RATIFY THEM IN ACCORDANCE WITH ARTICLE 110.

ARTICLE 4

1.  MEMBERSHIP IN THE UNITED FEDERATION IS OPEN TO ANY OTHER PEACEFUL PLANET-ARY SOCIAL SYSTEMS WHICH ACCEPT THE OBLIGATIONS CONTAINED IN THESE ARTICLES OF FEDERATION AND, IN THE JUDGEMENT OF THE FEDERATION, ARE CAPABLE AND WILL-ING TO CARRY OUT THESE OBLIGATIONS;

2.  THE ADMISSION OF ANY SUCH PLANETARY SOCIAL SYSTEM TO MEMBERSHIP IN THE UNITED FEDERATION OF PLANETS IS CONTINGENT UPON THE DECISION OF THE SUPREME ASSEMBLY UPON RECOMMENDATION OF THE FEDERATION COUNCIL.

ARTICLE 5

THE SUPREME ASSEMBLY MAY SUSPEND THE RIGHTS AND PRIVILEGES OF MEMBERSHIP OF ANY MEMBER OF THE UNITED FEDERATION AGAINST WHICH THE FEDERATION COUNCIL HAS TAKEN PREVENTIVE OR ENFORCEMENT ACTION.  THE FEDERATION COUNCIL MAY RESTORE THESE RIGHTS AND PRIVILEGES OF MEMBERSHIP AT ITS DISCRETION;

ARTICLES OF FEDERATION

## ARTICLE 6

ANY MEMBER OF THE UNITED FEDERATION WHICH HAS PERSISTENTLY VIOLATED THE PURPOSES AND PRINCIPLES CONTAINED IN THESE ARTICLES OF FEDERATION MAY BE EXPELLED FROM THE FEDERATION BY THE SUPREME ASSEMBLY UPON THE RECOMMENDATION OF THE FEDERATION COUNCIL.

# CHAPTER III
AGENCIES

## ARTICLE 7

1.  THERE ARE ESTABLISHED AS THE PRINCIPAL AGENCIES OF THE UNITED FEDERATION OF PLANETS:  A SUPREME ASSEMBLY, A FEDERATION COUNCIL, AN ECONOMIC AND SOCIAL COUNCIL, A TRUSTEESHIP COUNCIL, AN INTERPLANETARY SUPREME COURT OF JUSTICE, A STAR FLEET COMBINED PEACE-KEEPING FORCE, AND A SECRETARIAT;

2.  SUCH SUBSIDIARY AGENCIES AS MAY BE DEEMED NECESSARY FROM TIME TO TIME MAY BE ESTABLISHED IN ACCORDANCE WITH THESE ARTICLES OF FEDERATION;

## ARTICLE 8

THE UNITED FEDERATION SHALL PLACE NO RESTRICTION ON THE ELIGIBILITY OF MALE AND FEMALE LIFE-FORMS OF ANY MEMBER PLANETARY SOCIAL SYSTEM TO PARTICI-PATE IN ANY CAPACITY UNDER CONDITIONS OF EQUALITY IN ITS PRINCIPAL AND SUB-SIDIARY AGENCIES.

# CHAPTER IV
THE SUPREME ASSEMBLY

## ARTICLE 9
COMPOSITION

THE SUPREME ASSEMBLY SHALL CONSIST OF ALL THE MEMBERS OF THE UNITED FEDERATION OF PLANETS.  EACH MEMBER SHALL BE ENTITLED TO HAVE NOT MORE THAN FIVE (5) REPRESENTATIVES IN THIS BODY;

FUNCTIONS AND POWERS
## ARTICLE 10

THE SUPREME ASSEMBLY MAY DISCUSS ANY QUESTIONS ON ANY MATTERS WITHIN THE SCOPE OF THESE ARTICLES OF FEDERATION OR RELATING TO THE POWERS AND FUNCTIONS OF ANY AGENCIES PROVIDED FOR IN THESE ARTICLES OF FEDERATION AND, EXCEPT AS PROVIDED IN ARTICLE 12, MAY MAKE RECOMMENDATIONS TO THE MEMBERS AND THE FEDERATION COUNCIL OR BOTH ON ANY SUCH QUESTIONS OR MATTERS;

## ARTICLE 11

1.  THE SUPREME ASSEMBLY MAY CONSIDER THE GENERAL PRINCIPLES OF COOPERATION IN MAINTAINING INTERPLANETARY PEACE AND SECURITY, INCLUDING DISARMAMENT AND THE REGULATION OF ARMAMENTS, AND MAY MAKE RECOMMENDATIONS WITH REGARD TO SUCH PRINCIPLES TO THE MEMBERS OR THE FEDERATION COUNCIL OR TO BOTH;

2.  THE SUPREME ASSEMBLY MAY DISCUSS ANY QUESTIONS RELATIVE TO THE MAINTEN-ANCE OF INTRA-GALACTIC PEACE AND SECURITY PUT TO IT BY ANY MEMBER OR THE FEDERATION COUNCIL, OR A NON-MEMBER PLANETARY SOCIAL SYSTEM IN ACCORDANCE WITH ARTICLE 25 PARAGRAPH 2 AND, EXCEPT AS PROVIDED IN ARTICLE 12, MAY MAKE RECOMMENDATIONS WITH REGARD TO ANY SUCH QUESTIONS TO THE MEMBERS, THE FEDERATION COUNCIL, OR THE PLEADING PLANETARY SOCIAL SYSTEM, OR TO ALL OF THEM.  ANY SUCH QUESTION ON WHICH ACTION IS NECESSARY SHALL BE REFERRED TO THE FEDERATION COUNCIL BY THE SUPREME ASSEMBLY EITHER BEFORE OR AFTER DISCUSSION;

3.  THE SUPREME ASSEMBLY MAY CALL SITUATIONS WHICH ARE LIKELY TO ENDANGER THE INTERPLANETARY AND INTRA-GALACTIC PEACE AND SECURITY TO THE ATTENTION OF THE FEDERATION COUNCIL;

ARTICLES OF FEDERATION

4.  THE POWERS OF THE SUPREME ASSEMBLY AS SET FORTH IN THIS ARTICLE SHALL
NOT LIMIT THE SCOPE OF ARTICLE 10;

ARTICLE 12

1.  WHERE THE FEDERATION COUNCIL IS EXECUTING THE FUNCTIONS ASSIGNED TO IT
UNDER THESE ARTICLES OF FEDERATION WITH RESPECT TO ANY DISPUTE OR SITUATION,
THE SUPREME ASSEMBLY SHALL MAKE NO RECOMMENDATION WITH REGARD TO THAT DIS-
PUTE OR SITUATION UNLESS SO REQUESTED BY THE FEDERATION COUNCIL;

2.  THE SUPREME-SECRETARIAT, WITH THE CONSENT OF THE FEDERATION COUNCIL,
SHALL NOTIFY THE SUPREME ASSEMBLY AT EACH SESSION OF ANY MATTERS RELATING
TO THE MAINTENANCE OF INTERPLANETARY PEACE AND SECURITY WHICH ARE UNDER DIS-
CUSSION IN THE FEDERATION COUNCIL, AND SHALL NOTIFY THE SUPREME ASSEMBLY, OR
THE MEMBERS IF THE SUPREME ASSEMBLY IS NOT IN SESSION, IMMEDIATELY WHEN THE
FEDERATION COUNCIL COMPLETES ITS DELIBERATIONS ON ANY SUCH MATTERS;

ARTICLE 13

1.  THE SUPREME ASSEMBLY SHALL INITIATE STUDIES AND MAKE RECOMMENDATIONS FOR
THE PURPOSE OF:

   A)  PROMOTING INTERPLANETARY COOPERATION IN POLITICAL FIELDS AND ENCOURAG-
       ING THE PROGRESSIVE DEVELOPMENT OF INTERPLANETARY LAW AND ITS CODIFI-
       CATION;

   B)  PROMOTING INTERPLANETARY COOPERATION IN THE ECONOMIC, SOCIAL, CULTURAL,
       EDUCATIONAL, AND HEALTH FIELDS, AND ASSISTING IN THE REALIZATION OF
       INTELLIGENT LIFE-FORM RIGHTS AND FUNDAMENTAL FREEDOMS FOR ALL WITHOUT
       DISTINCTION AS TO CULTURE, SEX, LANGUAGE, OR RELIGION;

2.  THE FURTHER RESPONSIBILITIES, FUNCTIONS, AND POWERS OF THE SUPREME ASSEM-
BLY WITH RESPECT TO MATTERS MENTIONED IN PARAGRAPH 1(B) ABOVE ARE SET FORTH
IN CHAPTERS IX AND X;

ARTICLE 14

    SUBJECT TO THE PROVISIONS OF ARTICLE 12, THE SUPREME ASSEMBLY MAY RECOM-
MEND MEASURES FOR THE PEACEFUL ADJUSTMENT OF ANY SITUATION, REGARDLESS OF
ORIGIN, WHICH IT DEEMS LIKELY TO IMPAIR THE GENERAL WELFARE OR FRIENDLY RE-
LATIONS AMONG THE PLANETS, INCLUDING SITUATIONS RESULTING FROM VIOLATIONS OF
THE PROVISIONS OF THESE ARTICLES OF FEDERATION SETTING FORTH THE PURPOSES AND
PRINCIPLES OF THE UNITED FEDERATION OF PLANETS;

ARTICLE 15

1.  THE SUPREME ASSEMBLY SHALL RECEIVE AND CONSIDER REGULAR AND SPECIAL
REPORTS FROM THE FEDERATION COUNCIL; WHICH REPORTS SHALL INCLUDE AN ACCOUNT
OF THE MEASURES THAT THE FEDERATION COUNCIL HAS DECIDED UPON OR TAKEN TO
MAINTAIN INTERPLANETARY PEACE AND SECURITY;

2.  THE SUPREME ASSEMBLY SHALL RECEIVE AND CONSIDER REPORTS FROM THE OTHER
AGENCIES OF THE UNITED FEDERATION ON AGREED UPON REGULAR PERIODS OR REPORTING;

ARTICLE 16

    THE SUPREME ASSEMBLY SHALL PERFORM SUCH FUNCTIONS OF INTRA-GALACTIC
TRUSTEESHIP AS ARE ASSIGNED TO IT UNDER CHAPTERS XII AND XIII, INCLUDING THE
APPROVAL OF THE TRUSTEESHIP AGREEMENTS FOR AREAS WHICH ARE NOT DESIGNATED AS
STRATEGIC;

ARTICLE 17

1.  THE SUPREME ASSEMBLY SHALL CONSIDER AND APPROVE THE BUDGET OF THE UNITED
FEDERATION OF PLANETS;

2.  THE EXPENSES OF THE UNITED FEDERATION OF PLANETS SHALL BE BORNE BY THE
MEMBERS AS APPORTIONED BY THE SUPREME ASSEMBLY;

ARTICLES OF FEDERATION

3.   THE SUPREME ASSEMBLY SHALL CONSIDER AND APPROVE ANY FINANCIAL AND BUDGE-
TARY ARRANGEMENTS WITH SPECIALIZED AGENCIES REFERRED TO IN ARTICLE 57 AND
SHALL EXAMINE THE ADMINISTRATIVE BUDGETS OF SUCH SPECIALIZED AGENCIES WITH A
VIEW TO MAKING RECOMMENDATIONS TO THE AGENCIES CONCERNED;

4.   ALL BUDGETS OF, AND EXPENSES OF THE UNITED FEDERATION SHALL BE MADE AND
PAID IN THE COMMON INTERPLANETARY CREDIT.   THE COMMON INTERPLANETARY CREDIT
SHALL BE THE OFFICIAL MEDIUM OF EXCHANGE WITHIN THE UNITED FEDERATION TREATY
EXPLORATION TERRITORY;

VOTING
ARTICLE 18

1.   EACH MEMBER OF THE SUPREME ASSEMBLY SHALL HAVE ONE VOTE;

2.   DECISIONS OF THE SUPREME ASSEMBLY ON IMPORTANT QUESTIONS SHALL BE MADE
ON A TWO-THIRDS (2/3) MAJORITY VOTE OF THE MEMBERS PRESENT AND VOTING.   THESE
QUESTIONS SHALL INCLUDE:   RECOMMENDATIONS WITH RESPECT TO THE MAINTENANCE OF
INTERPLANETARY PEACE AND SECURITY; THE ELECTION OF NON-PERMANENT MEMBERS TO
THE FEDERATION COUNCIL; THE ELECTION OF MEMBERS OF THE TRUSTEESHIP COUNCIL IN
ACCORDANCE WITH PARAGRAPH 1(C) OF ARTICLE 86; THE ADMISSION OF NEW MEMBERS
TO THE FEDERATION; THE SUSPENSION OF THE RIGHTS AND PRIVILEGES OF MEMBER-
SHIP; THE EXPULSION OF MEMBERS; QUESTIONS RELATING TO THE OPERATION OF THE
TRUSTEESHIP SYSTEM; AND BUDGETARY QUESTIONS;

3.   DECISIONS ON OTHER QUESTIONS, INCLUDING THE DETERMINATION OF ADDITIONAL
CATEGORIES OF QUESTIONS TO BE DECIDED BY A TWO-THIRDS (2/3) MAJORITY, SHALL
BE MADE BY A MAJORITY VOTE OF THE MEMBERS PRESENT AND VOTING;

ARTICLE 19

    A MEMBER OF THE UNITED FEDERATION WHICH IS IN ARREARS IN THE PAYMENT OF
ITS FINANCIAL OBLIGATIONS TO THE FEDERATION SHALL HAVE NO VOTE IN THE
SUPREME ASSEMBLY IF THE AMOUNT IT IS IN ARREARS EQUALS OR EXCEEDS THE AMOUNT
OF THE CONTRIBUTIONS DUE FROM IT FOR THE PRECEDING TWO ACCOUNTING PERIODS.
THE SUPREME ASSEMBLY MAY, NEVERTHELESS, PERMIT SUCH A MEMBER TO VOTE IF IT IS
SATISFIED THAT THE FAILURE TO PAY IS DUE TO CONDITIONS BEYOND THE CONTROL OF
THE MEMBER.

PROCEDURE
ARTICLE 20

    THE SUPREME ASSEMBLY SHALL MEET IN REGULAR PERIODIC SESSIONS AND IN SUCH
SPECIAL SESSIONS AS OCCASION MAY REQUIRE.   SPECIAL SESSIONS SHALL BE CON-
VOKED BY THE SUPREME-SECRETARIAT AT THE REQUEST OF THE FEDERATION COUNCIL OR
OF A MAJORITY OF THE MEMBERS OF THE UNITED FEDERATION;

ARTICLE 21

    THE SUPREME ASSEMBLY SHALL ADOPT ITS OWN RULES OF PROCEDURE.   IT SHALL
ELECT ITS PRESIDENT FOR EACH SESSION;

ARTICLE 22

    THE SUPREME ASSEMBLY MAY ESTABLISH SUCH SUBSIDIARY AGENCIES AS IT DEEMS
NECESSARY FOR THE PERFORMANCE OF ITS FUNCTIONS.

## CHAPTER V
THE FEDERATION COUNCIL

ARTICLE 23
COMPOSITION

1.   THE FEDERATION COUNCIL SHALL CONSIST OF ELEVEN (11) MEMBERS OF THE UNI-
TED FEDERATION.   THE UNITED NATIONS OF THE PLANET EARTH, THE PLANETARY CON-
FEDERATION OF 40 ERIDANI, THE UNITED PLANETS OF 61 CYGNI, THE STAR EMPIRE
OF EPSILON INDII, AND THE ALPHA CENTAURI CONCORDIUM OF PLANETS SHALL BE
PERMANENT MEMBERS OF THE FEDERATION COUNCIL.   THE SUPREME ASSEMBLY SHALL

ARTICLES OF FEDERATION

ELECT SIX (6) OTHER MEMBERS OF THE UNITED FEDERATION TO BE NON-PERMANENT MEM-
BERS OF THE FEDERATION COUNCIL, DUE REGARD BEING ESPECIALLY PAID, IN THE
FIRST INSTANCE, TO THE CONTRIBUTION OF THE MEMBERS OF THE UNITED FEDERATION
TO THE MAINTENANCE OF INTERPLANETARY PEACE AND SECURITY AND TO THE OTHER
PURPOSES OF THE FEDERATION, AND ALSO TO EQUITABLE GEO-GALACTICAL DISTRIBU-
TION;

2.   THE NON-PERMANENT MEMBERS OF THE FEDERATION COUNCIL SHALL BE ELECTED FOR
A TERM OF TWO (2) SESSION PERIODS.  IN THE FIRST ELECTION OF NON-PERMANENT
MEMBERS, HOWEVER, THREE (3) SHALL BE ELECTED FOR A TERM OF ONE (1) SESSION
PERIOD.  A RETIRING MEMBER SHALL NOT BE ELIGIBLE FOR IMMEDIATE RE-ELECTION;

FUNCTIONS AND POWERS
ARTICLE 24

1.   IN ORDER TO ASSURE PROMPT AND EFFECTIVE ACTION BY THE UNITED FEDERATION
OF PLANETS, ITS MEMBERS CONFER ON THE FEDERATION COUNCIL PRIMARY RESPONSI-
BILITY FOR THE MAINTENANCE OF INTERPLANETARY PEACE AND SECURITY, AND AGREE
THAT IN CARRYING OUT ITS DUTIES UNDER THIS RESPONSIBILITY THE FEDERATION
COUNCIL ACTS ON THEIR BEHALF;

2.   IN DISCHARGING THESE DUTIES THE FEDERATION COUNCIL SHALL ACT IN ACCORD-
ANCE WITH THE PURPOSES AND PRINCIPLES OF THE UNITED FEDERATION.  THE SPECI-
FIC POWERS GRANTED TO THE FEDERATION COUNCIL FOR THE DISCHARGE OF THESE
DUTIES ARE LAID DOWN IN CHAPTERS VI, VII, VIII, AND XII;

3.   THE FEDERATION COUNCIL SHALL SUBMIT REGULAR AND, WHEN NECESSARY, SPECIAL
REPORTS TO THE SUPREME ASSEMBLY FOR ITS CONSIDERATION;

ARTICLE 25

     THE MEMBERS OF THE UNITED FEDERATION AGREE TO ACCEPT AND CARRY OUT THE
DECISIONS OF THE FEDERATION COUNCIL IN ACCORDANCE WITH THESE ARTICLES OF
FEDERATION;

ARTICLE 26

     IN ORDER TO PROMOTE THE ESTABLISHMENT AND MAINTENANCE OF INTERPLANETARY
PEACE AND SECURITY WITH THE LEAST DIVERSION OF THE FEDERATION'S LIFE-FORMS,
AND ECONOMIC RESOURCES FOR ARMAMENTS, THE FEDERATION COUNCIL SHALL BE
RESPONSIBLE FOR FORMULATING, WITH THE ASSISTANCE OF STAR FLEET HEADQUARTERS
STAFF REFERRED TO IN ARTICLE 47, PLANS TO BE SUBMITTED TO THE MEMBERS OF THE
UNITED FEDERATION FOR THE ESTABLISHMENT OF A SYSTEM FOR THE REGULATION OF
ARMAMENTS;

ARTICLE 27
VOTING

1.   EACH MEMBER OF THE FEDERATION COUNCIL SHALL HAVE ONE VOTE;

2.   DECISIONS OF THE FEDERATION COUNCIL ON PROCEDURAL MATTERS SHALL BE MADE
BY AN AFFIRMATIVE VOTE OF SEVEN (7) MEMBERS;

3.   DECISIONS OF THE FEDERATION COUNCIL ON ALL OTHER MATTERS SHALL BE MADE
ON AFFIRMATIVE VOTE OF SEVEN (7) MEMBERS INCLUDING THE CONCURRING VOTES OF
THE PERMANENT MEMBERS, PROVIDED THAT, IN DECISIONS UNDER CHAPTER VI, AND
UNDER PARAGRAPH 3 OF ARTICLE 52, A PARTY TO THE DISPUTE SHALL REFRAIN FROM
VOTING;

PROCEDURE
ARTICLE 28

1.   THE FEDERATION COUNCIL SHALL BE SO ORGANIZED AS TO BE ABLE TO FUNCTION
CONTINUOUSLY.  EACH MEMBER OF THE FEDERATION COUNCIL SHALL, FOR THIS PUR-
POSE, BE REPRESENTED AT ALL TIMES AT THE SEAT OF THE FEDERATION;

2.   THE FEDERATION COUNCIL SHALL HOLD PERIODIC MEETINGS AT WHICH EACH OF ITS
MEMBERS MAY, IF IT SO DESIRES, BE REPRESENTED BY A MEMBER OF ITS GOVERNMENT

ARTICLES OF FEDERATION

OR BY SOME OTHER SPECIALLY DESIGNATED REPRESENTATIVE;

3.   THE FEDERATION COUNCIL MAY HOLD MEETINGS AT SUCH PLACES OTHER THAN THE SEAT OF THE FEDERATION AS IN ITS JUDGEMENT WILL FACILITATE ITS WORK;

### ARTICLE 29

THE FEDERATION COUNCIL MAY ESTABLISH SUCH SUBSIDIARY AGENCIES AS IT DEEMS NECESSARY FOR THE PERFORMANCE OF ITS FUNCTIONS;

### ARTICLE 30

THE FEDERATION COUNCIL SHALL ADOPT ITS OWN RULES OF PROCEDURE, INCLUDING THE METHOD OF SELECTING ITS GOVERNOR;

### ARTICLE 31

ANY MEMBER OF THE UNITED FEDERATION WHICH IS NOT A MEMBER OF THE FEDERATION COUNCIL MAY PARTICIPATE, WITHOUT VOTE, IN THE DISCUSSION OF ANY QUESTION BROUGHT BEFORE THE FEDERATION COUNCIL WHENEVER THE LATTER CONSIDERS THAT THE INTERESTS OF THE MEMBER ARE SPECIFICALLY AFFECTED;

### ARTICLE 32

ANY MEMBER OF THE UNITED FEDERATION WHICH IS NOT A MEMBER OF THE FEDERATION COUNCIL OR ANY PLANETARY SOCIAL SYSTEM WHICH IS NOT A MEMBER OF THE UNITED FEDERATION OF PLANETS, IF IT IS A PARTY TO A DISPUTE UNDER CONSIDERATION BY THE FEDERATION COUNCIL, SHALL BE INVITED TO PARTICIPATE, WITHOUT VOTE, IN THE DISCUSSION RELATING TO THE DISPUTE.  THE FEDERATION COUNCIL SHALL LAY DOWN THE CONDITIONS AS IT DEEMS JUST FOR THE PARTICIPATION OF A PLANETARY SOCIAL SYSTEM WHICH IS NOT A MEMBER OF THE UNITED FEDERATION OF PLANETS.

## CHAPTER VI
PACIFIC SETTLEMENT OF DISPUTES

### ARTICLE 33

1.   THE PARTIES TO ANY DISPUTE, THE CONTINUANCE OF WHICH IS LIKELY TO ENDANGER THE MAINTENANCE OF INTERPLANETARY PEACE AND SECURITY, SHALL, FIRST OF ALL, SEEK A SOLUTION BY NEGOTIATION, ENQUIRY, MEDIATION, CONCILLIATION, ARBITRATION, JUDICIAL SETTLEMENT, RESORT TO REGIONAL AGENCIES OR ARRANGEMENTS, OR OTHER PEACEFUL MEANS OF THEIR OWN CHOICE;

2.   THE FEDERATION COUNCIL SHALL, WHEN IT DEEMS NECESSARY, CALL UPON THE PARTIES TO SETTLE THEIR DISPUTE BY SUCH MEANS;

### ARTICLE 34

THE FEDERATION COUNCIL MAY INVESTIGATE ANY DISPUTE, OR ANY SITUATION THAT MIGHT LEAD TO INTERPLANETARY FRICTION OR GIVE RISE TO A DISPUTE, IN ORDER TO DETERMINE WHETHER THE CONTINUANCE OF THE DISPUTE OR SITUATION IS LIKELY TO ENDANGER THE MAINTENANCE OF INTERPLANETARY PEACE AND SECURITY;

### ARTICLE 35

1.   ANY MEMBER OF THE UNITED FEDERATION MAY BRING ANY DISPUTE, OR ANY SITUATION OF THE NATURE REFERRED TO IN ARTICLE 34, TO THE ATTENTION OF THE FEDERATION COUNCIL OR THE SUPREME ASSEMBLY;

2.   A PLANETARY SOCIAL SYSTEM WHICH IS NOT A MEMBER OF THE UNITED FEDERATION OF PLANETS MAY BRING TO THE ATTENTION OF THE FEDERATION COUNCIL OR THE SUPREME ASSEMBLY ANY DISPUTE TO WHICH IT IS A PARTY IF IT ACCEPTS IN ADVANCE, FOR THE PURPOSES OF THE DISPUTE, THE OBLIGATION OF PACIFIC SETTLEMENT PROVIDED IN THESE ARTICLES OF FEDERATION;

3.   THE PROCEEDINGS OF THE SUPREME ASSEMBLY IN RESPECT TO MATTERS BROUGHT TO ITS ATTENTION UNDER THIS ARTICLE WILL BE SUBJECT TO THE PROVISIONS OF ARTICLES 11 AND 12;

ARTICLE 36                      ARTICLES OF FEDERATION

1.   THE FEDERATION COUNCIL MAY, AT ANY STAGE OF A DISPUTE OF THE NATURE REFERRED TO IN ARTICLE 33 OR OF A SITUATION OF LIKE NATURE, RECOMMEND PRO-CEDURES OR APPROPRIATE METHODS OF ADJUSTMENT;

2.   THE FEDERATION COUNCIL SHALL TAKE INTO CONSIDERATION ANY PROCEDURES FOR THE SETTLEMENT OF THE DISPUTE WHICH HAVE ALREADY BEEN ADOPTED BY THE PARTIES;

3.   IN MAKING RECOMMENDATIONS UNDER THE ARTICLE THE FEDERATION COUNCIL SHOULD ALSO TAKE INTO CONSIDERATION THAT LEGAL DISPUTES SHOULD AS A GENERAL RULE BE REFERRED TO THE INTERPLANETARY SUPREME COURT OF JUSTICE IN ACCORDANCE WITH THE PROVISIONS OF THE STATUTE OF THE COURT;

ARTICLE 37

1.   SHOULD THE PARTIES TO A DISPUTE AS REFERRED TO IN ARTICLE 33 FAIL TO SETTLE IT BY MEANS INDICATED IN THAT ARTICLE, THEY SHALL REFER IT TO THE FEDERATION COUNCIL;

2.   IF THE FEDERATION COUNCIL DEEMS THAT THE CONTINUANCE OF THE DISPUTE IS IN FACT LIKELY TO ENDANGER THE MAINTENANCE OF INTERPLANETARY PEACE AND SECURITY, IT SHALL DECIDE WHETHER TO TAKE ACTION UNDER ARTICLE 36 OR TO RECOMMEND SUCH TERMS AS IT MAY CONSIDER APPROPRIATE;

ARTICLE 38

   WITHOUT PREJUDICE TO THE PROVISIONS OF ARTICLES 33 TO 37, THE FEDERATION COUNCIL MAY, IF ALL THE PARTIES TO ANY DISPUTE SO REQUEST, MAKE RECOMMENDA-TIONS TO THE PARTIES WITH A VIEW TO A PACIFIC SETTLEMENT OF THE DISPUTE.

CHAPTER VII
ACTION WITH RESPECT TO THREATS TO THE PEACE,
BREACHES OF THE PEACE, AND ACTS OF AGGRESSION

ARTICLE 39

   THE FEDERATION COUNCIL SHALL DETERMINE THE EXISTENCE OF ANY THREAT TO THE PEACE, BREACH OF THE PEACE, OR ACT OF AGRESSION AND SHALL MAKE RECOMMENDATIONS TO MAINTAIN OR RESTORE INTERPLANETARY PEACE AND SECURITY;

ARTICLE 40

   IN ORDER TO PREVENT AGGRAVATION OF THE SITUATION, THE FEDERATION COUNCIL MAY CALL UPON THE PARTIES CONCERNED TO COMPLY WITH SUCH PROVISIONAL MEASURES AS IT DEEMS NECESSARY OR DESIRABLE.  SUCH PROVISIONAL MEASURES SHALL BE WITH-OUT PREJUDICE TO THE RIGHTS, CLAIMS, OR POSITION OF THE PARTIES CONCERNED. THE FEDERATION COUNCIL SHALL TAKE INTO ACCOUNT ANY FAILURE TO COMPLY WITH SUCH PROVISIONAL MEASURES;

ARTICLE 41

   THE FEDERATION COUNCIL MAY DECIDE WHAT MEASRUES SHORT OF THE USE OF ARMED FORCE ARE TO BE EMPLOYED TO GIVE EFFECT TO ITS DECISIONS, AND MAY CALL UPON THE MEMBERS OF THE UNITED FEDERATION TO APPLY SUCH MEASURES.  THESE MAY INCLUDE PARTIAL OR COMPLETE INTERRUPTION OF ECONOMIC RELATIONS, INTER-PLANET RADIO AND SPACE TRAVEL, AND SEVERANCE OF DIPLOMATIC RELATIONS;

ARTICLE 42

   SHOULD THE FEDERATION COUNCIL CONSIDER THAT MEASURES UNDER ARTICLE 41 WOULD BE INADEQUATE OR HAVE PROVED TO BE INADEQUATE, IT MAY TAKE SUCH ACTION BY ARMED FORCE AS NECESSARY TO MAINTAIN OR RESTORE INTERPLANETARY PEACE AND SECURITY.  SUCH ACTION MAY INCLUDE DEMONSTRATIONS, BLOCKADES, AND OTHER OPERATIONS BY STAR FLEET COMBINED PEACE-KEEPING FORCES;

ARTICLE 43

   ALL MEMBERS OF THE UNITED FEDERATION IN OBLIGATION TO THE MAINTENANCE OF INTERPLANETARY PEACE AND SECURITY, AGREE TO MAKE AVAILABLE TO STAR FLEET, ON

ARTICLES OF FEDERATION

CALL OF THE FEDERATION COUNCIL, ARMED FORCES, ASSISTANCE, AND FACILITIES, INCLUDING RIGHTS OF PASSAGE, NECESSARY FOR THE MAINTENANCE OF INTERPLANETARY PEACE AND SECURITY;

ARTICLE 44

WHEN THE FEDERATION COUNCIL HAS DECIDED TO USE FORCE IT SHALL, BEFORE CALLING UPON A MEMBER NOT REPRESENTED ON IT TO PROVIDE ARMED FORCES IN FUL-FILLMENT OF OBLIGATIONS ASSUMED UNDER ARTICLE 43, INVITE THAT MEMBER TO PARTICIPATE IN THE DECISIONS OF THE FEDERATION COUNCIL RELATING TO THE EMPLOYMENT OF CONTINGENTS OF THE MEMBER'S ARMED FORCES;

ARTICLE 45

IN ORDER TO ENABLE THE UNITED FEDERATION TO TAKE URGENT MILITARY MEAS-URES, ALL MEMBERS SO CAPABLE, SHALL ASSIGN CONTINGENTS OF THEIR ARMED FORCES TO STAR FLEET TO BE EMPLOYED AS A SINGLE PEACE-KEEPING FORCE OF THE UNITED FEDERATION OF PLANETS. ALL CONTINGENTS SO ASSIGNED, AND FOR THE DURATION OF THEIR ASSIGNMENT, SHALL HOLD FULL FAITH AND LOYALTY TO THE UNITED FEDERATION OF PLANETS AND THE PROTECTION OF THE PURPOSES AND PRINCIPLES OF THESE ARTI-CLES OF FEDERATION;

ARTICLE 46

PLANS FOR THE APPLICATION OF STAR FLEET ARMED FORCES SHALL BE MADE BY THE FEDERATION COUNCIL WITH THE ASSISTANCE OF THE MILITARY STAFF COMMITTEE OF STAR FLEET HEADQUARTERS;

ARTICLE 47

1. THERE SHALL BE ESTABLISHED WITHIN STAR FLEET A MILITARY STAFF COMMITTEE TO ADVISE AND ASSIST THE FEDERATION COUNCIL ON ALL MATTERS RELATING TO THE UNITED FEDERATION'S MILITARY REQUIREMENTS FOR MAINTAINING INTERPLANETARY PEACE AND SECURITY;

2. THE MILITARY STAFF COMMITTEE SHALL CONSIST OF THE CHIEFS OF STAFF OF THE PERMANENT MEMBERS OF THE FEDERATION COUNCIL, OR THEIR REPRESENTATIVES. ANY MEMBER OF THE UNITED FEDERATION MAY BE INVITED TO PROVIDE REPRESENTATION ON THE MILITARY STAFF COMMITTEE WHERE ITS RESPONSIBILITIES REQUIRES THE PARTICI-PATION OF THAT MEMBER IN ITS WORK;

3. THE MILITARY STAFF COMMITTEE, WITH THE AUTHORIZATION OF THE FEDERATION COUNCIL, SHALL ESTABLISH A STAR FLEET AS THE ARMED, PEACE-KEEPING, FORCES OF THE UNITED FEDERATION OF PLANETS. IT SHALL BE RESPONSIBLE FOR THE ESTABLISH-MENT AND MAINTENANCE OF ALL FACILITIES OF STAR FLEET, INCLUDING ARMED SHIPS, STARBASES, AND TRAINING FACILITIES;

4. THE MILITARY STAFF COMMITTEE SHALL BE RESPONSIBILE UNDER THE FEDERATION COUNCIL FOR THE STRATEGIC DIRECTION OF STAR FLEET ARMED FORCES, AND THE OTHER ARMED FORCES OF THE MEMBERS WHEN REQUIRED FOR THE MAINTENANCE OF INTER-PLANETARY PEACE AND SECURITY;

ARTICLE 48

THE ACTION REQUIRED TO CARRY OUT DECISIONS OF THE FEDERATION COUNCIL FOR THE MAINTENANCE OF INTERPLANETARY PEACE AND SECURITY SHALL BE TAKEN BY STAR FLEET, USING SUCH CONTINGENTS AS APPROPRIATE TO THE SPECIFIC ACTION;

ARTICLE 49

THE MEMBERS OF THE UNITED FEDERATION SHALL JOIN IN AFFORDING MUTUAL ASSISTANCE IN CARRYING OUT THE MEASURES DECIDED UPON BY THE FEDERATION COUNCIL AND IN ASSISTING STAR FLEET IN THE PERFORMANCE OF ITS DUTIES AND OBLIGATIONS;

ARTICLE 50

IF PREVENTIVE OR ENFORCEMENT MEASURES AGAINST ANY PLANET ARE TAKEN BY THE FEDERATION COUNCIL, ANY OTHER PLANET, WHETHER A MEMBER OF THE UNITED FEDERA-

ARTICLES OF FEDERATION

TION OR NOT, WHICH FINDS ITSELF CONFRONTED WITH SPECIAL ECONOMIC PROBLEMS ARISING FROM THE CARRYING OUT OF THESE MEASURES SHALL HAVE THE RIGHT TO CONSULT WITH THE FEDERATION COUNCIL WITH REGARD TO THE SOLUTION OF ITS PROBLEMS;

ARTICLE 51

NOTHING IN THESE ARTICLES OF FEDERATION SHALL IMPAIR THE INHERENT RIGHT OF INDIVIDUAL OR COLLECTIVE SELF-DEFENSE AGAINST ARMED ATTACKS OCCURRING TO MEMBERS OF THE UNITED FEDERATION, UNTIL THE FEDERATION COUNCIL HAS TAKEN MEASURES NECESSARY TO MAINTAIN INTERPLANETARY PEACE AND SECURITY, AND STAR FLEET FORCES CAN BE BROUGHT INTO ACTION. SUCH ACTIONS TAKEN BY MEMBERS OF THE UNITED FEDERATION IN THEIR SELF-DEFENSE SHALL BE IMMEDIATELY REPORTED TO THE FEDERATION COUNCIL.

## CHAPTER VIII
STAR FLEET

ARTICLE 52

1. THERE IS ESTABLISHED A STAR FLEET AS THE ARMED PEACE-KEEPING FORCES OF THE UNITED FEDERATION OF PLANETS. IT SHALL INITIALLY BE COMPRISED OF CONTINGENTS ASSIGNED TO IT BY MEMBERS OF THE UNITED FEDERATION UNDER ARTICLE 43 UNTIL SUCH TIME AS FACILITIES, RECRUITMENT, AND TRAINING OBVIATES THE NECESSITY OF DRAWING UPON THE ARMAMENT OF ANY MEMBER, EXCEPT AS PROVIDED IN ARTICLE 49;

2. THE OPERATIONS AND ACTIONS OF STAR FLEET SHALL AT ALL TIMES BE UNDER THE DIRECT COGNIZANCE OF THE FEDERATION COUNCIL AND THE MILITARY STAFF COMMITTEE WHICH SHALL ALSO PREPARE AND APPROVE THE BUDGET FOR STAR FLEET OPERATIONS;

3. INITIAL EXPENDITURE IS AUTHORIZED UNDER THESE ARTICLES OF FEDERATION FOR THE ESTABLISHMENT OF A STAR FLEET HEADQUARTERS AND TWO STARBASES TO BE EQUITABLY LOCATED WITHIN THE BOUNDARY OF THE UNITED FEDERATION OF PLANETS AND OUTSIDE OF ANY POSSIBLE CONFLICT WITH THE TERRITORIAL BOUNDARIES OF ANY MEMBER OF THE UNITED FEDERATION. THE FEDERATION COUNCIL SHALL REVIEW AND APPROVE SUCH OTHER EXPANSIONS OF STARBASES AND OTHER FACILITIES AS SHALL SEEM APPROPRIATE FROM TIME TO TIME IN THE MAINTENANCE OF INTERPLANETARY PEACE AND SECURITY;

4. INITIAL EXPENDITURE IS ALSO GRANTED UNDER THESE ARITCLES OF FEDERATION FOR THE ESTABLISHMENT OF A STAR FLEET ACADEMY FOR THE PURPOSE OF TRAINING OFFICERS AND PERSONNEL FOR STAR FLEET DUTY. THE STANDARDS FOR TRAINING SUCH OFFICERS AND PERSONNEL SHALL BE DETERMINED BY THE MILITARY STAFF COMMITTEE AND APPROVED BY THE FEDERATION COUNCIL;

ARTICLE 53

1. INITIAL EXPENDITURE IS GRANTED UNDER THESE ARTICLES OF FEDERATION FOR THE DESIGN, PROCUREMENT, AND OPERATION OF FOURTEEN (14) HEAVY CRUISER TYPE OF STARSHIPS TO PROVIDE THE NUCLEUS OF STAR FLEET'S PEACE-KEEPING ARMED FORCES. THESE CRUISERS SHALL BE CAPABLE OF EXTENDED DURATION PATROL OF INTRA-GALACTIC RANGE, WITH WEAPONRY APPROPRIATE TO SUCH CLASS OF STARSHIPS. THEY SHALL BE PROVIDED WITH FIRE-POWER SUPERIOR TO THAT NOW EMPLOYED BY ANY MEMBER OF THE UNITED FEDERATION, AND APPROPRIATE TO THE TASKS EXPECTED OF THEM;

2. EXPENDITURE IS ALSO GRANTED UNDER THESE ARTICLES OF FEDERATION FOR THE PROCUREMENT OR CONSTRUCTION OF SUCH LESSER CLASSES OF SPACE FORCES AS SHALL BE REQUIRED TO SUPPORT STAR FLEET OPERATIONS AND THE HEAVY CRUISER CLASS OF STARSHIPS. THESE MAY BE, BUT NOT NECESSARILY LIMITED TO, TYPES SUCH AS SCOUTS, DESTROYERS, TRANSPORTS, RE-SUPPLY, SHUTTLECRAFT, AND SURVEY SHIPS;

ARTICLE 54

1. THE TRAINING OF BASE PERSONNEL AND SHIP COMPLEMENTS SHALL INCLUDE ALL FIELDS OF SCIENCE AND TECHNOLOGY AS WELL AS THE MILITARY ARTS IN STAR FLEET. IT IS THE INTENT OF THESE ARTICLES OF FEDERATION THAT STAR FLEET SHALL BE

ARTICLES OF FEDERATION

USED TO CONDUCT MISSIONS OF SCIENTIFIC EXPLORATION AND INVESTIGATION WITHIN THE TREATY EXPLORATION TERRITORY WHENEVER ITS SERVICES ARE NOT REQUIRED IN THE MAINTENANCE OF INTERPLANETARY PEACE AND SECURITY;

2. STAR FLEET HEADQUARTERS AND THE FEDERATION COUNCIL SHALL BE AT ALL TIMES KEPT INFORMED OF THE ACTIVITIES UNDERTAKEN, OR CONTEMPLATED, FOR THE SCIENTIFIC EXPLORATION AND INVESTIGATION OF THE TREATY EXPLORATION TERRITORY. ANY SHIP SO EMPLOYED SHALL BE DETACHED FROM MILITARY FLEET DUTY AND RE-ASSIGNED AS A NON-MILITARY SCIENTIFIC UNIT OF THE UNITED FEDERATION.

## CHAPTER IX
INTERPLANETARY ECONOMIC
AND SOCIAL COOPERATION

### ARTICLE 55

WITH A VIEW TO CREATING CONDITIONS OF STABILITY AND WELL-BEING WHICH ARE NECESSARY FOR PEACEFUL RELATIONS AMONG PLANETARY SOCIAL SYSTEMS BASED ON RESPECT FOR THE PRINCIPLES OF EQUAL RIGHTS AND SELF-DETERMINATION OF ALL INTELLIGENT LIFE-FORMS, THE UNITED FEDERATION OF PLANETS SHALL PROMOTE:

A) HIGHER STANDARDS OF LIVING, FULL EMPLOYMENT, AND CONDITIONS OF ECONOMIC AND SOCIAL PROGRESS AND DEVELOPMENT;

B) SOLUTION OF INTERPLANETARY ECONOMIC, SOCIAL, HEALTH, AND RELATED PROBLEMS; AND INTERPLANETARY CULTURAL AND EDUCATIONAL COOPERATION; AND

C) UNIVERSAL RESPECT FOR, AND OBSERVANCE OF, INTELLIGENT LIFE-FORM RIGHTS AND FUNDAMENTAL FREEDOMS FOR ALL WITHOUT DISTINCTION AS TO CULTURE, SEX, LANGUAGE, OR RELIGION;

### ARTICLE 56

ALL MEMBERS PLEDGE THEMSELVES TO TAKE JOINT AND SEPARATE ACTION IN COOPERATION WITH THE UNITED FEDERATION FOR THE ACHIEVEMENT OF THE PURPOSES AND GOALS SET FORTH IN ARTICLE 55;

### ARTICLE 57

1. THE VARIOUS SPECIALIZED AGENCIES, ESTABLISHED BY INTERPLANETARY AGREEMENT AND HAVING WIDE INTERPLANETARY RESPONSIBILITIES AS DEFINED IN THEIR BASIC INSTRUMENTS IN ECONOMIC, SOCIAL, CULTURAL, EDUCATIONAL, HEALTH, AND RELATED FIELDS, SHALL BE BROUGHT INTO RELATIONSHIP WITH THE UNITED FEDERATION IN ACCORDANCE WITH ARTICLE 63;

2. SUCH AGENCIES THUS BROUGHT INTO RELATIONSHIP WITH THE UNITED FEDERATION ARE HEREAFTER REFERRED TO AS SPECIALIZED AGENCIES;

### ARTICLE 58

THE UNITED FEDERATION SHALL MAKE RECOMMENDATIONS FOR THE COORDINATION OF THE POLICIES AND ACTIVITIES OF THE SPECIALIZED AGENCIES;

### ARTICLE 59

THE UNITED FEDERATION SHALL, WHERE APPROPRIATE, INITIATE NEGOTIATIONS AMONG ITS MEMBERS CONCERNED FOR THE CREATION OF ANY NEW SPECIALIZED AGENCIES REQUIRED FOR THE ACCOMPLISHMENT OF THE PURPOSES SET FORTH IN ARTICLE 55;

### ARTICLE 60

RESPONSIBILITY FOR THE DISCHARGE OF THE FUNCTIONS OF THE UNITED FEDERATION AS SET FORTH IN THIS CHAPTER SHALL BE VESTED IN THE SUPREME ASSEMBLY AND, UNDER THE AUTHORITY OF THE SUPOREME ASSEMBLY, IN THE ECONOMIC AND SOCIAL COUNCIL WHICH SHALL HAVE FOR THIS PURPOSE THE POWERS SET FORTH IN CHAPTER X.

## CHAPTER X
THE ECONOMIC AND SOCIAL COUNCIL

ARTICLES OF FEDERATION

COMPOSITION
ARTICLE 61

1.  THE ECONOMIC AND SOCIAL COUNCIL SHALL CONSIST OF EIGHTEEN (18) MEMBERS OF THE UNITED FEDERATION AS ELECTED BY THE SUPREME ASSEMBLY;

2.  SUBJECT TO THE PROVISIONS OF PARAGRAPH 3, SIX (6) MEMBERS OF THE ECONOMIC AND SOCIAL COUNCIL SHALL BE ELECTED EACH SESSION PERIOD FOR A TERM OF THREE (3) SESSION PERIODS.  A RETIRING MEMBER SHALL BE ELIGIBLE FOR IMMEDIATE RE-ELECTION;

3.  AT THE FIRST ELECTION, EIGHTEEN (18) MEMBERS OF THE ECONOMIC AND SOCIAL COUNCIL SHALL BE CHOSEN, THE TERM OF OFFICE OF SIX (6) MEMBERS SO CHOSEN WILL EXPIRE AT THE END OF ONE (1) SESSION PERIOD, AND THE TERMS OF SIX (6) OTHER MEMBERS AT THE END OF TWO (2) SESSION PERIODS IN ACCORDANCE WITH ARRANGEMENTS MADE BY THE SUPREME ASSEMBLY;

4.  EACH MEMBER OF THE ECONOMIC AND SOCIAL COUNCIL SHALL HAVE ONE (1) REPRE-SENTATIVE;

FUNCTIONS AND POWERS
ARTICLE 62

1.  THE ECONOMIC AND SOCIAL COUNCIL MAY MAKE OR INITIATE STUDIES AND REPORTS WITH RESPECT TO INTERPLANETARY ECONOMIC, SOCIAL, CULTURAL, EDUCATIONAL, HEALTH, AND RELATED MATTERS AND MAY MAKE RECOMMENDATIONS WITH RESPECT TO ANY SUCH MATTERS TO THE SUPREME ASSEMBLY, TO THE MEMBERS OF THE UNITED FEDERATION, AND TO SPECIALIZED AGENCIES CONCERNED;

2.  IT MAY MAKE RECOMMENDATIONS FOR THE PURPOSE OF PROMOTING RESPECT FOR, AND OBSERVANCE OF, INTELLIGENT LIFE-FORM RIGHTS AND FUNDAMENTAL FREEDOMS FOR ALL;

3.  IT MAY PREPARE DRAFT INSTRUMENTS WITH THE RULES PRESCRIBED BY THE UNITED FEDERATION;

4.  IT MAY PREPARE DRAFT INSTRUMENTS FOR ADMISSION TO THE SUPREME ASSEMBLY, WITH RESPECT TO MATTERS FALLING WITHIN ITS COMPETENCE;

5.  IT MAY CALL, IN ACCORDANCE WITH THE RULES PRESCRIBED BY THE UNITED FEDERA-TION, INTERPLANETARY CONFERENCES ON MATTERS FALLING WITHIN ITS COMPETENCE;

ARTICLE 63

1.  THE ECONOMIC AND SOCIAL COUNCIL MAY ENTER INTO AGREEMENTS WITH ANY OF ITS AGENCIES REFERRED TO IN ARTICLE 57, DEFINING THE TERMS ON WHICH THE AGENCY CONCERNED SHALL BE BROUGHT INTO RELATIONSHIP WITH THE UNITED FEDERATION.  SUCH AGREEMENTS SHALL BE SUBJECT TO APPROVAL BY THE SUPREME ASSEMBLY;

2.  IT MAY COORDINATE THE ACITIVITIES OF THE SPECIALIZED AGENCIES THROUGH CON-SULTATION WITH AND RECOMMENDATIONS TO SUCH AGENCIES AND THROUGH RECOMMENDA-TIONS TO THE SUPREME ASSEMBLY AND TO THE MEMBERS OF THE UNITED FEDERATION;

ARTICLE 64

THE ECONOMIC AND SOCIAL COUNCIL MAY TAKE APPROPRIATE STEPS TO OBTAIN REPORTS FROM THE SPECIALIZED AGENCIES.  IT MAY MAKE ARRANGEMENTS WITH THE MEMBERS OF THE UNITED FEDERATION AND WITH THE SPECIALIZED AGENCIES TO OBTAIN REPORTS ON THE STEPS TAKEN TO GIVE EFFECT TO ITS OWN RECOMMENDATIONS AND TO RECOMMENDATIONS ON MATTER FALLING WITHIN ITS COMPETENCE BY THE SUPREME ASSEMBLY;

ARTICLE 65

THE ECONOMIC AND SOCIAL COUNCIL MAY FURNISH INFORMATION TO THE FEDERATION COUNCIL AND SHALL ASSIST THE FEDERATION COUNCIL UPON ITS REQUEST;

ARTICLE 66

1.  THE ECONOMIC AND SOCIAL COUNCIL SHALL PERFORM SUCH FUNCTIONS AS FALL

ARTICLES OF FEDERATION

WITHIN ITS COMPETENCE IN CONNECTION WITH THE CARRYING OUT OF THE RECOMMENDA-
TIONS OF THE SUPREME ASSEMBLY;

2.   IT MAY, WITH THE APPROVAL OF THE SUPREME ASSEMBLY, PERFORM SERVICES AT
THE REQUEST OF MEMBERS OF THE UNITED FEDERATION AND AT THE REQUEST OF SPECIAL-
IZED AGENCIES;

3.   IT SHALL PERFORM SUCH OTHER FUNCTIONS AS ARE SPECIFIED ELSEWHERE IN THESE
ARTICLES OF FEDERATION OR AS MAY BE ASSIGNED TO IT BY THE SUPREME ASSEMBLY;

VOTING
ARTICLE 67

1.   EACH MEMBER OF THE ECONOMIC AND SOCIAL COUNCIL SHALL HAVE ONE VOTE;

2.   DECISIONS OF THE ECONOMIC AND SOCIAL COUNCIL SHALL BE MADE BY A MAJORITY
OF THE MEMBERS PRESENT AND VOTING;

PROCEDURES
ARTICLE 68

THE ECONOMIC AND SOCIAL COUNCIL SHALL SET UP COMMISSIONS IN ECONOMIC AND
SOCIAL FIELDS AND FOR THE PROMOTION OF INTELLIGENT LIFE-FORM RIGHTS, AND SUCH
OTHER COMMISSIONS AS MAY BE REQUIRED FOR THE PERFORMANCE OF ITS FUNCTIONS;

ARTICLE 69

THE ECONOMIC AND SOCIAL COUNCIL SHALL INVITE ANY MEMBER OF THE UNITED
FEDERATION TO PARTICIPATE, WITHOUT VOTE, IN ITS DELIBERATIONS ON ANY MATTER
OF PARTICULAR CONCERN TO THAT MEMBER;

ARTICLE 70

THE ECONOMIC AND SOCIAL COUNCIL MAY MAKE ARRANGEMENTS FOR REPRESENTATIVES
OF THE SPECIALIZED AGENCIES TO PARTICIPATE, WITHOUT VOTE, IN ITS DELIBERATIONS
AND IN THOSE COMMISSIONS ESTABLISHED BY IT, AND FOR ITS REPRESENTATIVES TO
PARTICIPATE IN THE DELIBERATIONS OF THE SPECIALIZED AGENCIES;

ARTICLE 71

THE ECONOMIC AND SOCIAL COUNCIL MAY MAKE SUITABLE ARRANGEMENTS FOR CON-
SULTATION WITH NON-GOVERNMENTAL INTRA-PLANET ORGANIZATIONS WHICH ARE CONCERN-
ED WITH MATTERS WITHIN ITS COMPETENCE.   SUCH ARRANGEMENTS MAY BE MADE WITH
INTERPLANETARY ORGANIZATIONS AND, WHERE APPROPRIATE, WITH PLANETARY ORGANIZA-
TIONS AFTER CONSULTATION WITH MEMBERS OF THE UNITED FEDERATION CONCERNED;

ARTICLE 72

1.   THE ECONOMIC AND SOCIAL COUNCIL SHALL ADOPT ITS OWN RULES OF PROCEDURE,
INCLUDING THE METHOD OF SELECTING ITS DIRECTOR;

2.   THE ECONOMIC AND SOCIAL COUNCIL SHALL MEET AS REQUIRED IN ACCORDANCE WITH
ITS RULES, WHICH SHALL INCLUDE PROVISION FOR THE CONVENING OF MEETINGS ON THE
REQUEST OF A MAJORITY OF ITS MEMBERS.

## CHAPTER XI
DECLARATION REGARDING NON-
SELF-GOVERNING REGIONS

ARTICLE 73

MEMBERS OF THE UNITED FEDERATION WHICH HAVE ASSUMED RESPONSIBILITIES FOR
THE ADMINISTRATION OF REGIONS WHOSE INTELLIGENT LIFE-FORMS HAVE NOT YET
ATTAINED A FULL MEASURE OF SELF-GOVERNMENT RECOGNIZE THE PRINCIPLE THAT THE
INTERESTS OF THE INHABITANTS OF THESE REGIONS ARE PARAMOUNT, AND ACCEPT AS A
SACRED TRUST THE OBLIGATION TO PROMOTE TO THE UTMOST, WITHIN THE SYSTEM OF
INTERPLANETARY PEACE AND SECURITY ESTABLISHED BY THESE ARTICLES OF FEDERATION,
THE WELL-BEING OF THE INHABITANTS OF THESE REGIONS, AND, TO THIS END:

   A)   TO ENSURE, WITH DUE RESPECT FOR THE CULTURES OF THE INTELLIGENT LIFE-

ARTICLES OF FEDERATION

FORMS CONCERNED, THEIR POLITICAL, ECONOMIC, SOCIAL, AND EDUCATIONAL ADVANCEMENT, THEIR JUST TREATMENT, AND THEIR PROTECTION AGAINST ABUSES;

B) TO DEVELOP SELF-GOVERNMENT, TO TAKE DUE ACCOUNT OF THE POLITICAL ASPIRATIONS OF THE INTELLIGENT LIFE-FORMS, AND TO ASSIST THEM IN THE PROGRESSIVE DEVELOPMENT OF THEIR FREE POLITICAL INSTITUTIONS, ACCORDING TO THE PARTICULAR CIRCUMSTANCES OF EACH REGION AND ITS INTELLIGENT LIFE-FORMS AND THEIR VARYING STAGES OF ADVANCEMENT;

C) TO FURTHER INTERPLANETARY PEACE AND SECURITY;

D) TO PROMOTE CONSTRUCTIVE MEASURES OF DEVELOPMENT, TO ENCOURAGE RE-SEARCH, AND TO COOPERATE WITH ONE-ANOTHER AND, WHEN AND WHERE APPROPRIATE, WITH SPECIALIZED INTERPLANETARY BODIES WITH A VIEW TO THE PRACTICAL ACHIEVEMENT OF THE SOCIAL, ECONOMIC, AND SCIENTIFIC PURPOSES SET FORTH IN THIS ARTICLE; AND

E) TO TRANSMIT REGULARLY TO THE SUPREME-SECRETARIAT FOR INFORMATION PURPOSES, SUBJECT TO SUCH LIMITATIONS AS SECURITY AND STATUTORY CONSIDERATIONS MAY REQUIRE, STATISTICAL AND OTHER INFORMATION OF A TECHNICAL NATURE RELATING TO ECONOMIC, SOCIAL, AND EDUCATIONAL CONDITIONS IN THE REGIONS FOR WHICH THEY ARE RESPECTIVELY RESPONSI-BLE OTHER THAN THOSE REGIONS TO WHICH CHAPTER XII AND XIII APPLY;

ARTICLE 74

MEMBERS OF THE UNITED FEDERATION ALSO AGREE THAT THEIR POLICY IN RESPECT OF THE REGIONS TO WHICH THIS CHAPTER APPLIES, NO LESS THAN IN RESPECT OF THEIR METROPLOITAN AREAS, MUST BE BASED ON THE GENERAL PRINCIPLE OF GOOD-NEIGHBORLINESS, DUE ACCOUNT BEING TAKEN OF THE INTERESTS AND WELL-BEING OF THE REST OF THE FEDERATION TERRITORY IN SOCIAL, ECONOMIC, AND COMMERICIAL MATTERS.

CHAPTER XII
INTERPLANETARY TRUSTEESHIP SYSTEM

ARTICLE 75

THE UNITED FEDERATION SHALL ESTABLISH UNDER ITS AUTHORITY AN INTERPLANET-ARY TRUSTEESHIP SYSTEM FOR THE ADMINISTRATION AND SUPERVISION OF SUCH REGIONS AS MAY BE PLACED THEREUNDER BY SUBSEQUENT INIDIVIDUAL AGREEMENTS. THESE REGIONS ARE HEREINAFTER REFERRED TO AS TRUST REGIONS;

ARTICLE 76

THE BASIC OBJECTIVES OF THE TRUSTEESHIP SYSTEM, IN ACCORDANCE WITH THE PURPOSES AND PRINCIPLES OF THE UNITED FEDERATION AS LAID DOWN IN THESE ARTICLES OF FEDERATION, SHALL BE:

A) TO FURTHER INTERPLANETARY PEACE AND SECURITY;

B) TO PROMOTE THE POLITICAL, ECONOMIC, SOCIAL, AND EDUCATIONAL ADVANCE-MENT OF THE INHABITANTS OF THE TRUST REGIONS, AND THEIR PROGRESSIVE DEVELOPMENT TOWARDS SELF-GOVERNMENT OR INDEPENDENCE AS MAY BE APPRO-PRIATE TO THE PARTICULAR CIRCUMSTANCES OF EACH REGION AND ITS INTELLI-GENT LIFE-FORMS CONCERNED, AND AS MAY BE PROVIDED BY THE TERMS OF THE TRUSTEESHIP AGREEMENT;

C) TO ENCOURAGE RESPECT FOR INTELLIGENT LIFE-FORM RIGHTS AND FOR FUNDA-MENTAL FREEDOMS FOR ALL WITHOUT DISTINCTION AS TO CULTURE, SEX, LANGUAGE, OR RELIGION, AND TO ENCOURAGE RECOGNITION OF THE INTER-DEPENDENCE OF THE INTELLIGENT LIFE-FORMS OF THE GALAXY; AND

D) TO ENSURE EQUAL TREATMENT IN SOCIAL, ECONOMIC, AND COMMERCIAL MATTERS FOR ALL MEMBERS OF THE UNITED FEDERATION AND THEIR NATIONALS, AND ALSO

## ARTICLES OF FEDERATION

EQUAL TREATMENT FOR THE LATTER IN THE ADMINISTRATION OF JUSTICE, WITH-
OUT PREJUDICE TO THE ADJUSTMENT OF THE FOREGOING OBJECTIVES AND SUB-
JECT TO THE PROVISIONS OF ARTICLE 80;

### ARTICLE 77

1.   THE TRUSTEESHIP SYSTEM SHALL APPLY TO SUCH REGIONS IN THE FOLLOWING CATE-
GORIES AS MAY BE PLACED THEREUNDER BY MEANS OF TRUSTEESHIP AGREEMENTS:

A)   REGIONS NOW HELD UNDER MANDATE;

B)   REGIONS WHICH MAY BE DETACHED FROM ALIEN SOCIAL SYSTEMS AS A RESULT OF
INTERPLANETARY WAR; AND

C)   REGIONS VOLUNTARILY PLACED UNDER THE TRUSTEESHIP SYSTEM BY SOCIAL
SYSTEMS RESPONSIBLE FOR THEIR ADMINISTRATION;

2.   IT WILL BE A MATTER FOR SUBSEQUENT AGREEMENT AS TO WHICH REGIONS IN THE
FOREGOING CATEGORIES WILL BE BROUGHT UNDER THE TRUSTEESHIP SYSTEM AND UPON
WHAT TERMS;

### ARTICLE 78

THE TRUSTEESHIP SYSTEM SHALL NOT APPLY TO REGIONS WHICH HAVE BECOME MEM-
BERS OF THE UNITED FEDERATION OF PLANETS, RELATIONSHIP AMONG WHICH SHALL BE
BASED ON THE RESPECT FOR THE PRINCIPLE OF SOVERIEGN EQUALITY;

### ARTICLE 79

THE TERMS OF TRUSTEESHIP FOR EACH REGION TO BE PLACED UNDER THE TRUSTEE-
SHIP SYSTEM, INCLUDING ANY ALTERATION OR AMENDMENT, SHALL BE AGREED UPON BY
THE SOCIAL SYSTEMS DIRECTLY CONCERNED, INCLUDING THE MANDATORY POWER IN THE
CASE OF REGIONS HELD UNDER MANDATE BY A MEMBER OF THE UNITED FEDERATION, AND
SHALL BE APPROVED AS PROVIDED FOR IN ARTICLES 83 AND 85;

### ARTICLE 80

1.   EXCEPT AS MAY BE AGREED UPON IN INDIVIDUAL TRUSTEESHIP AGREEMENTS, MADE
UNDER ARTICLES 77, 79, AND 81, PLACING EACH REGION UNDER THE TRUSTEESHIP SYS-
TEM, AND UNTIL SUCH AGREEMENTS HAVE BEEN CONCLUDED, NOTHING IN THIS CHAPTER
SHALL BE CONSTRUED IN OR OF ITSELF TO ALTER IN ANY MANNER THE RIGHTS WHATSO-
EVER OF ANY SOCIAL SYSTEMS OR ANY INTELLIGENT LIFE-FORMS OR THE TERMS OF
EXISTING AGREEMENTS TO WHICH MEMBERS OF THE UNITED FEDERATION MAY RESPECTIVE-
LY BE PARTIES;

2.   PARAGRAPH 1 OF THIS ARTICLE SHALL NOT BE INTERPRETED AS GIVING GROUNDS
FOR DELAY OR POSTPONEMENT OF THE NEGOTIATION AND CONCLUSION OF AGREEMENTS FOR
PLACING MANDATED AND OTHER REGIONS UNDER THE TRUSTEESHIP SYSTEM AS PROVIDED
FOR IN ARTICLE 77;

### ARTICLE 81

THE TRUSTEESHIP AGREEMENT SHALL IN EACH CASE INCLUDE THE TERMS UNDER WHICH
THE TRUST REGION WILL BE ADMINISTERED AND DESIGNATE THE AUTHORITY WHICH WILL
BE EXERCISING THE ADMINISTRATION OF THE TRUST REGION.   SUCH AUTHORITY HEREIN-
AFTER CALLED THE ADMINISTERING AUTHORITY, MAY BE ONE OR MORE SOCIAL SYSTEMS
OF THE UNITED FEDERATION ITSELF;

### ARTICLE 82

THERE MAY BE DESIGNATED, IN THE TRUSTEESHIP AGREEMENT, A STRATEGIC AREA
OR AREAS WHICH MAY INCLUDE PART OR ALL OF THE TRUST REGION TO WHICH THE AGREE-
MENT APPLIES, WITHOUT PREJUDICE TO ANY SPECIAL AGREEMENT OR AGREEMENTS MADE
UNDER ARTICLE 43;

### ARTICLE 83

1.   ALL FUNCTIONS OF THE UNITED FEDERATION RELATING TO STRATEGIC AREAS, IN-

ARTICLES OF FEDERATION

CLUDING THE APPROVAL OF THE TERMS OF THE TRUSTEESHIP AGREEMENTS AND OF THEIR SUBSEQUENT ALTERATION OR AMENDMENT, SHALL BE EXERCISED BY THE FEDERATION COUNCIL;

2. THE BASIC PRINCIPLES SET FORTH IN ARTICLE 76 SHALL APPLY TO THE INTELLI-GENT LIFE-FORMS OF EACH STRATEGIC AREA;

3. THE FEDERATION COUNCIL SHALL, SUBJECT TO THE PROVISIONS OF THE TRUSTEESHIP AGREEMENTS AND WITHOUT PREJUDICE TO SECURITY CONSIDERATIONS, AVAIL ITSELF OF THE ASSISTANCE OF THE TRUSTEESHIP COUNCIL TO PERFORM THOSE FUNCTIONS OF THE UNITED FEDERATION UNDER THE TRUSTEESHIP SYSTEM RELATING TO POLITICAL, ECONOMIC, SOCIAL, AND EDUCATIONAL MATTERS IN THE STRATEGIC AREAS;

ARTICLE 84

IT SHALL BE THE DUTY OF THE ADMINISTERING AUTHORITY TO ENSURE THAT THE TRUST REGION SHALL PLAY ITS PART IN THE MAINTENANCE OF INTERPLANETARY PEACE AND SECURITY. TO THIS END THE ADMINISTERING AUTHORITY MAY MAKE USE OF VOLUN-TEER FORCES, FACILITIES, AND ASSISTANCE FROM THE TRUST REGION IN CARRYING OUT THE OBLIGATIONS TOWARDS THE FEDERATION COUNCIL UNDERTAKEN IN THIS REGARD BY THE ADMINISTERING AUTHORITY, AS WELL AS FOR THE LOCAL DEFENSE AND THE MAINTEN-ANCE OF LAW AND ORDER WITHIN THE TRUST REGION;

ARTICLE 85

1. THE FUNCTIONS OF THE UNITED FEDERATION WITH REGARD TO TRUSTEESHIP AGREE-MENTS FOR ALL REGIONS NOT DESIGNATED AS STRATEGIC, INCLUDING THE APPROVAL OF THE TERMS OF THE TRUSTEESHIP AGREEMENTS AND THEIR ALTERATION OR AMENDMENT, SHALL BE EXERCISED BY THE SUPREME ASSEMBLY;

2. THE TRUSTEESHIP COUNCIL, OPERATING UNDER THE AUTHORITY OF THE SUPREME ASSEMBLY, SHALL ASSIST THE SUPREME ASSEMBLY IN CARRYING OUT THESE FUNCTIONS.

# CHAPTER XIII
THE TRUSTEESHIP COUNCIL

COMPOSITION
ARTICLE 86

1. THE TRUSTEESHIP COUNCIL SHALL CONSIST OF THE FOLLOWING MEMBERS OF THE UNITED FEDERATION:

A) THOSE MEMBERS ADMINISTERING TRUST REGIONS;

B) SUCH OF THOSE MEMBERS MENTIONED BY NAME IN ARTICLE 23 AS ARE NOT ADMINISTERING TRUST REGIONS; AND

C) AS MANY OTHER MEMBERS ELECTED FOR THREE (3) SESSION PERIODS BY THE SUPREME ASSEMBLY AS MAY BE NECESSARY TO ENSURE THAT THE TOTAL NUMBER OF MEMBERS OF THE TRUSTEESHIP COUNCIL IS EQUALLY DIVIDED BETWEEN THOSE MEMBERS OF THE UNITED FEDERATION WHICH ADMINISTER TRUST REGIONS AND THOSE WHICH DO NOT;

2. EACH MEMBER OF THE TRUSTEESHIP COUNCIL SHALL DESIGNATE ONE (1) SPECIALLY QUALIFIED INTELLIGENT LIFE-FORM TO REPRESENT IT THEREIN;

FUNCTIONS AND POWERS
ARTICLE 87

THE SUPREME ASSEMBLY AND, UNDER ITS AUTHORITY, THE TRUSTEESHIP COUNCIL, IN CARRYING OUT THEIR FUNCTIONS, MAY:

A) CONSIDER REPORTS SUBMITTED BY THE ADMINISTERING AUTHORITY;

B) ACCEPT PETITIONS AND EXAMINE THEM IN CONSULTATION WITH THE ADMINISTER-ING AUTHORITY;

C) PROVIDE FOR PERIODIC VISITS TO THE RESPECTIVE TRUST REGIONS AT TIMES AGREED UPON WITH THE ADMINISTERING AUTHORITY; AND

ARTICLES OF FEDERATION

D) TAKE THESE AND OTHER ACTIONS IN CONFORMITY WITH THE TERMS OF THE TRUSTEESHIP AGREEMENTS;

### ARTICLE 88

THE TRUSTEESHIP COUNCIL SHALL FORMULATE A QUESTIONAIRE ON THE POLITICAL, ECONOMIC, SOCIAL, AND EDUCATIONAL ADVANCEMENT OF THE INHABITANTS OF EACH TRUST REGION, AND THE ADMINISTERING AUTHORITY FOR EACH TRUST REGION WITHIN THE COMPETENCE OF THE SUPREME ASSEMBLY SHALL MAKE A PERIODIC REPORT TO THE SUPREME ASSEMBLY UPON THE BASIS OF SUCH QUESTIONAIRE;

### VOTING
### ARTICLE 89

1. EACH MEMBER OF THE TRUSTEESHIP COUNCIL SHALL HAVE ONE VOTE;

2. DECISIONS OF THE TRUSTEESHIP COUNCIL SHALL BE MADE BY A MAJORITY OF THE MEMBERS PRESENT AND VOTING;

### PROCEDURE
### ARTICLE 90

1. THE TRUSTEESHIP COUNCIL SHALL ADOPT ITS OWN RULES OF PROCEDURE, INCLUD-ING THE METHOD OF SELECTING ITS DIRECTOR;

2. THE TRUSTEESHIP COUNCIL SHALL MEET AS REQUIRED IN ACCORDANCE WITH ITS RULES WHICH SHALL INCLUDE PROVISION FOR THE CONVENING OF MEETINGS ON THE REQUEST OF A MAJORITY OF ITS MEMBERS;

### ARTICLE 91

THE TRUSTEESHIP COUNCIL SHALL, WHEN APPROPRIATE, AVAIL ITSELF OF THE ASSISTANCE OF THE ECONOMIC AND SOCIAL COUNCIL AND OF THE SPECIALIZED AGENCIES IN REGARD TO MATTERS WITH WHICH THEY ARE RESPECTIVELY CONCERNED.

## CHAPTER XIV
### THE INTERPLANETARY SUPREME
### COURT OF JUSTICE

### ARTICLE 92

THE INTERPLANETARY SUPREME COURT OF JUSTICE SHALL BE THE PRINCIPAL JUDICIAL INSTRUMENT OF THE UNITED FEDERATION OF PLANETS. IT SHALL FUNCTION IN ACCORDANCE WITH THE APPENDED STATUTE, WHICH IS BASED UPON THE STATUTE OF THE TRIBUNALS OF ALPHA III, AND FORMS AN INTEGRAL PART OF THESE ARTICLES OF FEDERATION;

### ARTICLE 93

1. ALL MEMBERS OF THE UNITED FEDERATION ARE 'IPSO FACTO' PARTIES TO THE STATUTE OF THE INTERPLANETARY SUPREME COURT OF JUSTICE;

2. A SOCIAL SYSTEM WHICH IS NOT A MEMBER OF THE UNITED FEDERATION MAY BECOME A PARTY TO THE STATUTE OF THE INTERPLANETARY SUPREME COURT OF JUSTICE ON CONDITIONS TO BE DETERMINED IN EACH CASE BY THE SUPREME ASSEMBLY UPON THE RECOMMENDATION OF THE FEDERATION COUNCIL;

### ARTICLE 94

1. EACH MEMBER OF THE UNITED FEDERATION UNDERTAKES TO COMPLY WITH THE DECI-SION OF THE INTERPLANETARY SUPREME COURT OF JUSTICE IN ANY CASE TO WHICH IT IS A PARTY;

2. IF ANY PARTY TO A CASE FAILS TO PERFORM THE OBLIGATIONS INCUMBENT UPON IT UNDER A JUDGEMENT RENDERED BY THE COURT, THE OTHER PARTY MAY HAVE RECOURSE TO THE FEDERATION COUNCIL, WHICH MAY, IF IT DEEMS NECESSARY, MAKE RECOMMENDATIONS OR DECIDE UPON MEASURES TO BE TAKEN TO GIVE EFFECT TO THE JUDGEMENT;

### ARTICLE 95

NOTHING IN THESE ARTICLES OF FEDERATION SHALL PREVENT MEMBERS OF THE

ARTICLES OF FEDERATION

UNITED FEDERATION OF PLANETS FROM ENTRUSTING THE SOLUTION OF THEIR DIFFER-
ENCES TO OTHER TRIBUNALS BY VIRTUE OF AGREEMENTS ALREADY IN EXISTENCE OR
WHICH MAY BE CONCLUDED IN THE FUTURE;

ARTICLE 96

1.   THE SUPREME ASSEMBLY OR THE FEDERATION COUNCIL MAY REQUEST THE INTERPLANET-
ARY SUPREME COURT OF JUSTICE TO GIVE AN ADVISORY OPINION ON ANY LEGAL QUESTION;

2.   OTHER BODIES OF THE UNITED FEDERATION AND THE SPECIALIZED AGENCIES, WHICH
MAY AT ANY TIME BE SO AUTHORIZED BY THE SUPREME ASSEMBLY, MAY ALSO REQUEST
ADVISORY OPINIONS OF THE COURT ON LEGAL QUESTIONS ARISING WITHIN THE SCOPE OF
THEIR ACTIVITIES.

## CHAPTER XV
### THE SUPREME-SECRETARIAT

ARTICLE 97

THE SECRETARIAT SHALL BE COMPRISED OF A SUPREME-SECRETARIAT AND SUCH STAFF
AS THE UNITED FEDERATION MAY REQUIRE.   THE SUPREME-SECRETRAIAT SHALL BE
APPOINTED BY THE SUPREME ASSEMBLY UPON THE RECOMMENDATION OF THE FEDERATION
COUNCIL, AND SHALL BE THE CHIEF ADMINISTRATIVE OFFICER OF THE UNITED FEDERATION;

ARTICLE 98

THE SUPREME-SECRETARIAT SHALL ACT IN THAT CAPACITY IN ALL MEETINGS OF THE
SUPREME ASSEMBLY, OF THE FEDERATION COUNCIL, OF THE ECONOMIC AND SOCIAL
COUNCIL, AND OF THE TRUSTEESHIP COUNCIL, AND SHALL PERFORM SUCH OTHER FUNCTIONS
AS ARE ENTRUSTED TO THE SECRETARIAT BY THESE BODIES.   THE SUPREME-SECRETARIAT
SHALL MAKE A PERIODIC REPORT TO THE SUPREME ASSEMBLY ON THE WORK OF THE
UNITED FEDERATION OF PLANETS;

ARTICLE 99

THE SUPREME-SECRETARIAT MAY BRING TO THE ATTENTION OF THE FEDERATION
COUNCIL ANY MATTER WHICH IN HIS OPINION MAY THREATEN THE MAINTENANCE OF INTER-
PLANETARY PEACE AND SECURITY;

ARTICLE 100

1.   IN THE PERFORMANCE OF THEIR DUTIES THE SUPREME-SECRETARIAT AND THE STAFF
SHALL NOT SEEK OR RECEIVE INSTRUCTIONS FROM ANY GOVERNMENT OR FROM ANY OTHER
AUTHORITY EXTERNAL TO THE UNITED FEDERATION OF PLANETS.   THEY SHALL REFRAIN
FROM ANY ACTION WHICH MIGHT REFLECT ON THEIR POSITIONS AS INTERPLANETARY
OFFICIALS RESPONSIBLE ONLY TO THE UNITED FEDERATION;

2.   EACH MEMBER OF THE UNITED FEDERATION UNDERTAKES TO RESPECT THE EXCLUSIVE-
LY INTERPLANETARY CHARACTER OF THE RESPONSIBILITIES OF THE SUPREME-SECRETARIAT
AND THE STAFF AND SHALL NOT SEEK TO INFLUENCE THEM IN THE DISCHARGE OF THEIR
RESPONSIBILITIES;

ARTICLE 101

1.   THE STAFF SHALL BE APPOINTED BY THE SUPREME-SECRETARIAT UNDER REGULATIONS
ESTABLISHED BY THE SUPREME ASSEMBLY;

2.   APPROPRIATE STAFFS SHALL BE PERMANENTLY ASSIGNED TO THE ECONOMIC AND
SOCIAL COUNCIL, THE TRUSTEESHIP COUNCIL, AND, AS REQUIRED, TO OTHER BODIES OF
THE UNITED FEDERATION.   THESE STAFFS SHALL FORM A PART OF THE SECRETARIAT;

3.   THE PARAMOUNT CONSIDERATION IN THE EMPLOYMENT OF THE STAFF AND IN THE
DETERMINATION OF THE CONDITIONS OF SERVICE SHALL BE THE NECESSITY OF SECURING
THE HIGHEST STANDARDS OF EFFICIENCY, COMPETENCE, AND INTEGRITY.   DUE REGARD
SHALL BE PAID TO THE IMPORTANCE OF RECRUITING THE STAFF ON AS WIDE A GEO-
GALACTICAL BASIS AS POSSIBLE.

## CHAPTER XVI
MISCELANEOUS PROVISIONS

ARTICLES OF FEDERATION

### ARTICLE 102

1. EVERY TREATY AND EVERY INTERPLANETARY AGREEMENT ENTERED INTO BY ANY MEMBER OF THE UNITED FEDERATION AFTER THESE ARTICLES OF FEDERATION COME INTO FORCE SHALL AS SOON AS POSSIBLE BE REGISTERED WITH THE SUPREME-SECRETARIAT AND PUBLISHED BY HIM;

2. NO PARTY TO ANY SUCH TREATY OR INTERPLANETARY AGREEMENT WHICH HAS NOT BEEN REGISTERED IN ACCORDANCE WITH THE PROVISIONS OF PARAGRAPH 1 OF THIS ARTICLE MAY INVOKE THAT TREATY OR AGREEMENT BEFORE ANY BODY OF THE UNITED FEDERATION;

### ARTICLE 103

IN THE EVENT OF A CONFLICT BETWEEN THE OBLIGATIONS OF THE MEMBERS OF THE UNITED FEDERATION UNDER THESE ARTICLES OF FEDERATION AND THEIR OBLIGATIONS UNDER ANY OTHER INTERPLANETARY AGREEMENT, THEIR OBLIGATIONS UNDER THESE ARTI-CLES OF FEDERATION SHALL PREVAIL;

### ARTICLE 104

THE UNITED FEDERATION SHALL ENJOY IN THE TERRITORY OF EACH OF ITS MEMBERS SUCH LEGAL CAPACITY AS MAY BE NECESSARY FOR THE EXERCISE OF ITS FUNCTIONS AND THE FULFILLMENT OF ITS PURPOSES;

### ARTICLE 105

1. THE UNITED FEDERATION SHALL ENJOY IN THE TERRITORY OF EACH OF ITS MEMBERS SUCH PRIVILEGES AND IMMUNITIES AS ARE NECESSARY FOR THE FULFILLMENT OF ITS PURPOSES;

2. REPRESENTATIVES OF THE MEMBERS OF THE UNITED FEDERATION AND OFFICIALS OF THE ORGANIZATION SHALL SIMILARLY ENJOY SUCH PRIVILEGES AND IMMUNITIES AS ARE NECESSARY FOR THE INDEPENDENT EXERCISE OF THEIR FUNCTIONS IN CONNECTION WITH THE ORGANIZATION;

3. THE SUPREME ASSEMBLY MAY MAKE RECOMMENDATIONS WITH A VIEW TO DETERMINING THE DETAILS OF THE APPLICATION OF PARAGRAPHS 1 AND 2 OF THIS ARTICLE OR MAY PROPOSE CONVENTIONS TO THE MEMBERS OF THE UNITED FEDERATION FOR THIS PURPOSE.

## CHAPTER XVII
TRANSITORY SECURITY ARRANGEMENTS

### ARTICLE 106

1. PENDING THE COMING INTO FULL FORCE OF SUCH SPECIAL AGREEMENTS REFERRED TO IN ARTICLE 43 AS IN THE OPINION OF THE FEDERATION COUNCIL ENABLE IT TO BEGIN THE EXERCISE OF ITS RESPONSIBILITIES UNDER ARTICLE 42, THE PARTIES TO THE DECLARATION OF THE UNITED FEDERATION SHALL CONSULT WITH ONE ANOTHER AND THE OTHER MEMBERS OF THE UNITED FEDERATION WITH A VIEW TO SUCH JOINT ACTION ON BEHALF OF THE ORGANIZATION AS MAY BE NECESSARY FOR THE PURPOSE OF MAINTAINING INTERPLANETARY PEACE AND SECURITY;

2. NOTHING IN THESE ARTICLES OF FEDERATION SHALL INVALIDATE OR PRECLUDE ACTION IN RELATION TO ANY SOCIAL SYSTEM WHICH HAS BEEN AN ADVERSARY OF ANY SIGNATORY TO THESE ARTICLES OF FEDERATION, TAKEN OR AUTHORIZED AS A RESULT OF THAT WAR BY THE GOVERNMENTS HAVING RESPONSIBILITY FOR SUCH ACTION;

### ARTICLE 107

AMENDMENTS TO THESE ARTICLES OF FEDERATION SHALL COME INTO FORCE FOR ALL MEMBERS OF THE UNITED FEDERATION WHEN THEY HAVE BEEN ADOPTED BY A TWO-THIRDS (2/3) VOTE OF THE MEMBERS OF THE SUPREME ASSEMBLY AND RATIFIED IN ACCORDANCE WITH THEIR RESPECTIVE STATUTORY PROCESSES BY TWO-THIRDS (2/3) OF THE MEMBERS OF THE UNITED FEDERATION, INCLUDING ALL THE PERMANENT MEMBERS OF THE FEDERA-TION COUNCIL;

ARTICLES OF FEDERATION

ARTICLE 108

1. A GENERAL CONFERENCE OF THE MEMBERS OF THE UNITED FEDERATION FOR THE PUR-
POSE OF REVIEWING THESE ARTICLES OF FEDERATION MAY BE HELD AT A DATE AND
PLACE TO BE FIXED BY A TWO-THIRDS (2/3) VOTE OF THE MEMBERS OF THE SUPREME
ASSEMBLY AND BY A VOTE OF ANY SEVEN (7) MEMBERS OF THE FEDERATION COUNCIL.
EACH MEMBER OF THE UNITED FEDERATION SHALL HAVE ONE (1) VOTE IN THE CONFERENCE;

2. ANY ALTERATIONS OF THESE ARTICLES OF FEDERATION RECOMMENDED BY A TWO-
THIRDS (2/3) VOTE OF THE CONFERENCE SHALL TAKE EFFECT WHEN RATIFIED IN ACCORD-
ANCE WITH THEIR RESPECTIVE STATUTORY PROCESSES BY TWO-THIRDS (2/3) OF THE
MEMBERS OF THE UNITED FEDERATION INCLUDING ALL THE PERMANENT MEMBERS OF THE
FEDERATION COUNCIL;

3. IF SUCH CONFERENCE HAS NOT BEEN HELD BEFORE THE TENTH REGULAR SESSION OF
THE SUPREME ASSEMBLY FOLLOWING THE COMING INTO FORCE OF THESE ARTICLES OF
FEDERATION, THE PROPOSAL TO CALL SUCH A CONFERENCE SHALL BE PLACED ON THE
AGENDA OF THAT SESSION OF THE SUPREME ASSEMBLY, AND THE CONFERENCE SHALL BE
HELD IF SO DECIDED BY A MAJORITY VOTE OF THE MEMBERS OF THE SUPREME ASSEMBLY
AND BY A VOTE OF ANY SEVEN (7) MEMBERS OF THE FEDERATION COUNCIL.

## CHAPTER XVIII
RATIFICATION AND SIGNATURE

ARTICLE 109

1. THESE ARTICLES OF FEDERATION SHALL BE RATIFIED BY THE SIGNATORY GOVERN-
MENTS IN ACCORDANCE WITH THEIR RESPECTIVE STATUTORY PROCESSES;

2. THE RATIFICATIONS SHALL BE DEPOSITED WITH THE GOVERNMENT OF THE UNITED
NATIONS OF THE PLANET EARTH, WHICH SHALL NOTIFY ALL OF THE SIGNATORY GOVERN-
MENTS OF EACH DEPOSIT AS WELL AS THE SUPREME-SECRETARIAT OF THE ORGANIZATION
WHEN HE HAS BEEN APPOINTED;

3. THESE ARTICLES OF FEDERATION SHALL COME INTO FULL FORCE UPON THE DEPOSIT
OF THE RATIFICATIONS BY THE UNITED NATIONS OF THE PLANET EARTH, THE PLANETARY
CONFEDERATION OF 40 ERIDANI, THE UNITED PLANETS OF 61 CYGNI, THE STAR EMPIRE
OF EPSILON INDII, THE ALPHA CENTAURI CONCORDIUM OF PLANETS, AND BY A MAJORITY
OF THE OTHER SIGNATORY SOCIAL SYSTEMS. A PROTOCOL OF THE RATIFICATIONS
DEPOSITED SHALL THEREUPON BY DRAWN UP BY THE GOVERNMENT OF THE UNITED NATIONS
WHICH SHALL COMMUNICATE COPIES THEREOF TO ALL OF THE SIGNATORY GOVERNMENTS;

4. THE GOVERNMENTS SIGNATORY TO THESE ARTICLES OF FEDERATION WHICH RATIFY
IT AFTER IT HAS COME INTO FORCE WILL BECOME ORIGINAL MEMBERS OF THE UNITED
FEDERATION ON THE DATE OF THE DEPOSIT OF THEIR RESPECTIVE RATIFICATIONS;

ARTICLE 110

THESE ARTICLES OF FEDERATION, OF WHICH THE VARIOUS LANGUAGE TEXTS ARE
EQUALLY AUTHENTIC, UPON THE COMING INTO FULL FORCE OF THE UNITED FEDERATION
OF PLANETS, SHALL BE TRANSFERRED BY THE UNITED NATIONS TO THE ORGANIZATION
FOR PERMANENT DEPOSIT IN ITS ARCHIVES. DULY CERTIFIED COPIES THEREOF SHALL
BE TRANSMITTED BY THE SUPREME-SECRETARIAT TO THE GOVERNMENTS OF ALL THE
SIGNATORY SOCIAL SYSTEMS.

IN FAITH WHEREOF THE REPRESENTATIVES OF THE GOVERNMENTS OF THE UNITED FEDERA-
TION OF PLANETS HAVE SIGNED THESE ARTICLES OF FEDERATION.

DONE AT THE PLANET BABEL STARDATE 0965

(FOLLOWED BY THE SIGNATURE SHEETS OF THE
ORIGINAL SIGNATORY GOVERNMENTS)

# TREATY OF PEACE

BETWEEN THE **ROMULAN STAR EMPIRE**
AND THE **UNITED FEDERATION OF PLANETS**

NEGOTIATED BY SUBSPACE COMMUNICATION STARDATE 1200.5

**PART I** THE TERMS AND CONDITIONS HAVING BEEN NEGOTIATED AND AGREED TO BE IDENTICALLY UNDERSTOOD, THE ROMULAN STAR EMPIRE AND THE UNITED FEDERATION OF PLANETS MUTUALLY PLEDGE TO EACH OTHER THEIR SOLEMN WORD TO IMMEDIATELY CEASE HOSTILITIES BETWEEN THE TWO PARTIES EFFECTIVE STARDATE 1200.5;

**PART II** BETWEEN THE ADJACENT TERRITORIAL BOUNDARIES OF THE TWO PARTIES THERE IS ESTABLISHED A NEUTRAL ZONE, SEVEN HUNDRED AND FIFTY PARSECS IN WIDTH IN THE GALACTIC LONGITUDINAL PLANE, AND EXTENDING TO THE OUTER BOUNDARY OF THE GALAXY IN THE VERTICAL PLANE;

**PART III** ALL PERSONS AND FACILITIES OF ANY MANNER WHATSOEVER IDENTIFIABLE WITH EITHER PARTY SHALL BE IMMEDIATELY REMOVED FROM THIS ZONE. EFFECTIVE STARDATE 1210, NO PERSONS OR FACILITIES OF ANY MANNER WHATSOEVER IDENTIFIABLE WITH EITHER PARTY SHALL THEREAFTER BY INTRUDED INTO THIS ZONE. THE ROMULAN STAR EMPIRE AND THE UNITED FEDERATION OF PLANETS MUTUALLY PLEDGE TO EACH OTHER TO FAITHFULLY MAINTAIN THE NEUTRALITY OF THIS ZONE THEREAFTER;

**PART IV** ANY INTRUSION WHATSOEVER BY ANY PERSON OR FACILITY IDENTIFIABLE WITH EITHER PARTY INTO THIS NEUTRAL ZONE SHALL BE CONSIDERED TO BE A HOSTILE ACTION AND BREACH OF THIS PEACE. IN SUCH EVENT AN IMMEDIATE STATE OF WAR SHALL BE DECLARED TO EXIST BETWEEN THE ROMULAN STAR EMPIRE AND THE UNITED FEDERATION OF PLANETS; EXCEPT ONLY WHERE:

**PART V** SUCH INTRUSION BY ANY PERSON OR FACILITY IDENTIFIABLE WITH EITHER PARTY CAN BE UNDENIABLY DEMONSTRATED TO BE THE ACCIDENTAL RESULT OF CONDITIONS BEYOND THE CONTROL OF THAT PERSON OR THAT FACILITY AND DID, IN FACT, OCCUR WITHOUT HOSTILE INTENT;

**PART VI** TO THIS END, AND FOR PURPOSES OF MUTUAL MAINTENANCE OF THIS TREATY OF PEACE AND THIS NEUTRAL ZONE, THE ROMULAN STAR EMPIRE AND THE UNITED FEDERATION OF PLANETS AGREE TO KEEP OPEN AND MAINTAIN A CONSTANT SURVEILLANCE OF, SUBSPACE COMMUNICATION FREQUENCY K;

**PART VII** I, PRAETOR KARZAN, HAVING READ THE TERMS OF THIS TREATY VERBATIM OVER SUBSPACE COMMUNICATION FREQUENCY K, AND BEING IDENTIFIABLE BY VOICEPRINT OF THIS TRANSMISSION, DO HEREBY CERTIFY THAT I AM PRAETOR OF THE ROMULAN STAR EMPIRE WITH FULL POWERS TO EXECUTE THIS TREATY ON BEHALF OF THE EMPIRE;

**PART VIII** I, CRISTOFUR THORPE, HAVING READ THE TERMS OF THIS TREATY VERBATIM OVER SUBSPACE COMMUNICATION FREQUENCY K, AND BEING IDENTIFIABLE BY VOICEPRINT OF THIS TRANSMISSION, DO HEREBY CERTIFY THAT I AM GOVERNOR OF THE FEDERATION COUNCIL OF THE UNITED FEDERATION OF PLANETS WITH FULL POWERS TO EXECUTE THIS TREATY ON BEHALF OF THIS GOVERNMENT.

# TREATY OF PEACE
## IMPOSED BY ORGANIA STARDATE 3199.5

CONDITION 1:

THIS TREATY OF PEACE IS SIMULTANEOUSLY IMPOSED UPON THE KLINGON
EMPIRE AND THE UNITED FEDERATION OF PLANETS.  UNLESS YOUR GOVERN-
MENTS AND COMBATANTS IN GALACTIC SPACE AGREE TO AN IMMEDIATE
CESSATION OF HOSTILITIES, YOUR ARMED FORCES WHEREVER THEY MAY BE
WILL BE IMMEDIATELY DISABLED;

CONDITION 2:

HENCEFORTH FROM THIS TIME, WITHIN A ZONE SEVEN HUNDRED AND FIFTY
PARSECS IN WIDTH BETWEEN THE ADJACENT TERRITORIAL BOUNDARIES OF
BOTH PARTIES, NO ARMED HOSTILITIES MAY TAKE PLACE BETWEEN THE
KLINGON EMPIRE AND THE UNITED FEDERATION OF PLANETS;

CONDITION 3:

AT ANY TIME, SHOULD A PERSON OR UNIT OF EITHER PARTY ATTEMPT TO
ACT OR USE WEAPONRY IN A HOSTILE MANNER AGAINST THE PERSON OR A
UNIT OF THE OTHER PARTY WITHIN THIS ZONE, THAT PERSON OR UNIT,
AND THAT WEAPONRY, SHALL BE RENDERED IMMEDIATELY HARMLESS;

CONDITION 4:

THE TIME WILL COME IN THE FUTURE WHEN THE KLINGON EMPIRE AND THE
UNITED FEDERATION OF PLANETS WILL BECOME ALLIES AND GOOD FRIENDS,
WORKING TOGETHER IN PEACE AND HARMONY FOR THE BETTERMENT OF BOTH.
UNTIL THAT TIME, NEITHER PARTY MAY DENY TO THE OTHER PEACEFUL
ACCESS TO ITS PLANETARY BASES WITHIN THE NEUTRAL ZONE FOR SHORE
LEAVE, REST, AND REHABILITATION;

CONDITION 5:

BOTH PARTIES WILL RESPECT THE TERRITORIAL INTEGRITY OF ORGANIA AND
WILL MAKE NO FURTHER ATTEMPT TO INTRUDE INTO OUR PLANET'S TERRI-
TORY OR AFFAIRS.  WHEN THE TIME ARRIVES IN THE FUTURE FOR US TO
JOIN WITH BOTH PARTIES IN THE PEACEFUL DEVELOPMENT OF INTRA-
GALACTIC RELATIONS, WE WILL MAKE KNOWN TO YOU OUR INTENTIONS;

CONDITION 6:

WE ARE AWARE THAT, WITHIN THE NEUTRAL ZONE, THERE ARE MANY PLANETARY
SUB-CULTURES IN VARIOUS LEVELS OF EVOLUTIONARY DEVELOPMENT WHICH
COULD BENEFIT FROM THE ADVANCED CULTURES OF THE KLINGON EMPIRE AND
THE UNITED FEDERATION OF PLANETS.  TO THIS END, ORGANIA WILL PERMIT
SUCH PEACEFUL DEVELOPMENT AND, IN EACH SPECIFIC CASE, WILL AWARD
SUCH RIGHTS TO THE PARTY WHICH DEMONSTRATES IT CAN MOST EFFICIENTLY
DEVELOP THE PLANET TO THE BENEFIT OF ITS SOCIAL SYSTEMS.

FOR **ORGANIA**:

AYELBORNE
CLAYMARE
TREFAYNE

# UNITED FEDERATION
OF PLANETS - M-O GALAXY

## BANNER

B/W AS SHOWN
OFFICIAL COLORS:

☐ RED   N° SF10UC
■ SILVER N° SF01UC

# UNITED FEDERATION
## OF PLANETS - M-0 GALAXY

## SEAL

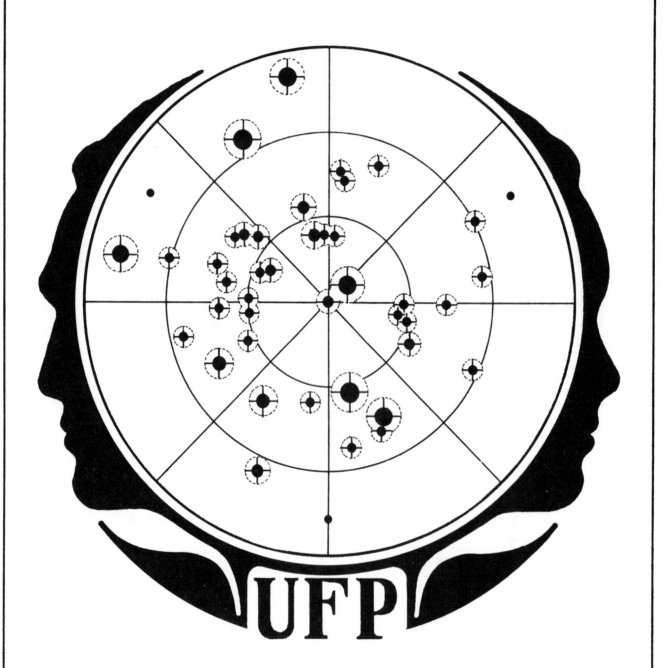

# UNITED NATIONS
PLANET EARTH - SOL SYSTEM

## FLAG

OFFICIAL GARRISON PROPORTIONS

B/W AS SHOWN
OFFICIAL COLORS:
☐ SKY BLUE N°SF16UC
■ SILVER N°SF01UC

OFFICIAL PARADE PROPORTIONS

# UNITED NATIONS
### PLANET EARTH - SOL SYSTEM

## SEAL

B/W AS SHOWN
OFFICIAL COLORS:
 SKY BLUE N°SF16UC
SILVER   N°SF01UC

# STAR FLEET TECHNICAL ORDER

# PLANETARY CONFEDERATION
OF 40 ERIDANI

## BANNER

B/W AS SHOWN
OFFICIAL COLORS:

| | | | |
|---|---|---|---|
| SKY BLUE Nº SF 16UC | | RED Nº SF 10UC | |
| ORANGE Nº SF 11UC | | INDIGO Nº SF 19UC | |

# PLANETARY CONFEDERATION
## OF 40 ERIDANI

## SIGNAT

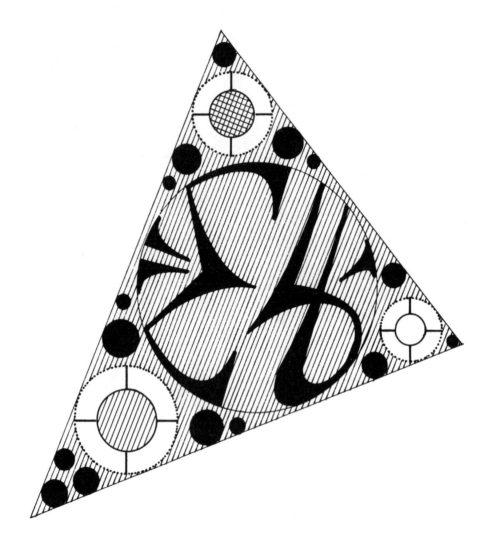

BLACK & WHITE AS SHOWN
OFFICIAL COLORS:

 SKY BLUE № SF 16 UC
ORANGE № SF 11 UC
RED № SF 10 UC
INDIGO № SF 19 UC

# UNITED PLANETS
## OF 61 CYGNI

## SHIELD*

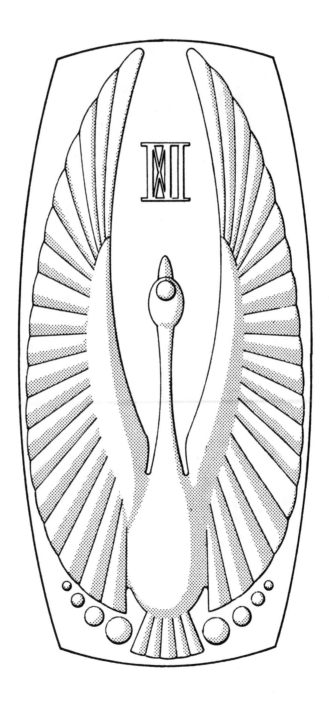

B/W AS SHOWN
OFFICIAL COLORS:
COPPER № SF05UC

*EQUIVALENT OF A FLAG, RAISED TOOLING
ON DOUBLE CONVEX CYGNUSIUM SHIELD

# UNITED PLANETS
OF 61 CYGNI

## ARMS

B/W AS SHOWN
OFFICIAL COLORS:

| | |
|---|---|
| | YELLOW Nº SF12UC |
| | ORANGE Nº SF11UC |
| | RED Nº SF10UC |
| | COPPER Nº SF05UC |

# STAR EMPIRE
OF EPSILON INDII

## STANDARD

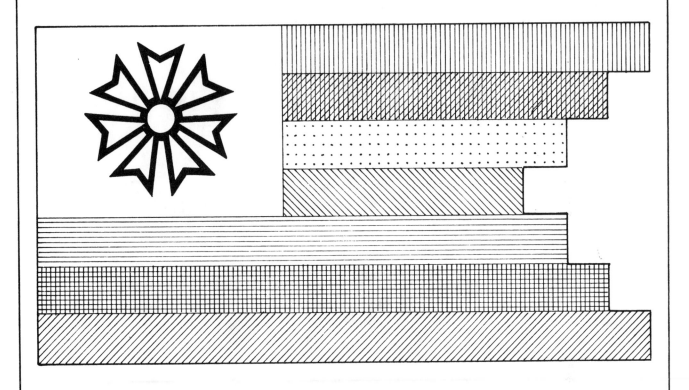

**B/W AS SHOWN**
OFFICIAL COLORS:

| | | |
|---|---|---|
| WHITE | N°SF06UC |
| RED | N°SF10UC |
| ORANGE | N°SF11UC |
| YELLOW | N°SF12UC |
| GREEN | N°SF15UC |
| GOLD | N°SF03UC |
| BLUE | N°SF18UC |
| INDIGO | N°SF19UC |
| VIOLET | N°SF21UC |

# STAR EMPIRE
## OF EPSILON INDII

## SEAL

**B/W AS SHOWN**
**OFFICIAL COLORS:**

| | | |
|---|---|---|
| WHITE | Nº SF 06 UC | |
| RED | Nº SF 10 UC | |
| ORANGE | Nº SF 11 UC | |
| YELLOW | Nº SF 12 UC | |
| GREEN | Nº SF 15 UC | |

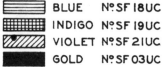

| | |
|---|---|
| BLUE | Nº SF 18 UC |
| INDIGO | Nº SF 19 UC |
| VIOLET | Nº SF 21 UC |
| GOLD | Nº SF 03 UC |

# ALPHA CENTAURI
## CONCORDIUM OF PLANETS

## PENNANT

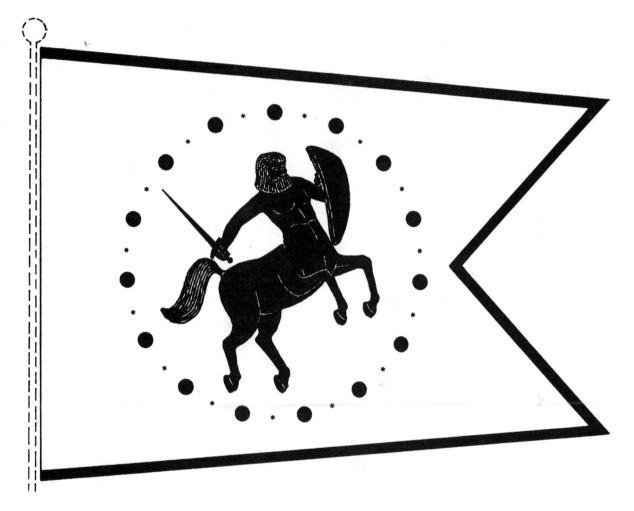

B/W AS SHOWN

OFFICIAL COLORS:

PURPLE N°SF26UC
GOLD N°SF03UC

# ALPHA CENTAURI
CONCORDIUM OF PLANETS

## ARMS

B/W AS SHOWN
OFFICIAL COLORS:

| | | |
|---|---|---|
| | PURPLE | №SF26UC |
| | YELLOW | №SF12UC |
| | ORANGE | №SF11UC |
| | RED | №SF10UC |
| | GOLD | №SF03UC |

# OFFICIAL TYPE STYLE
STAR FLEET SPECIFICATION

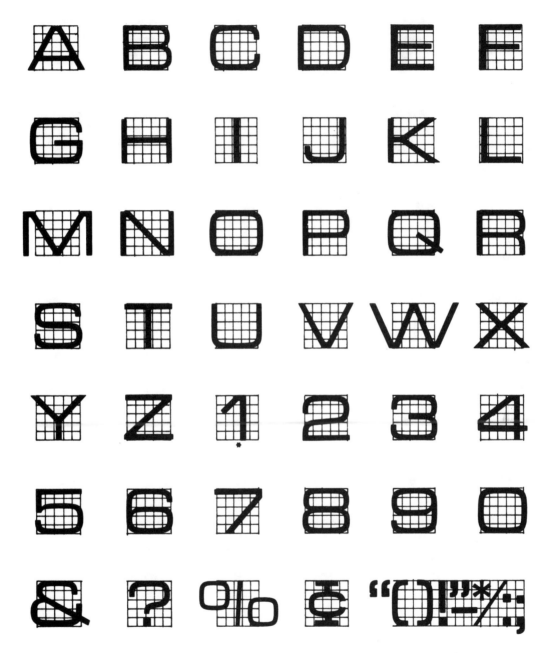

TYPICAL SPACING:

COMMON UNITED NATIONS LANGUAGE FORM.   EARTH FONT NAME: **Microgramma Ext.**

*DO NOT USE "1" IN FLEET OPERATIONS, INSTRUMENTATION, OR SHIP DESIGNATIONS.

# OFFICIAL TYPE STYLE
STAR FLEET SPECIFICATION

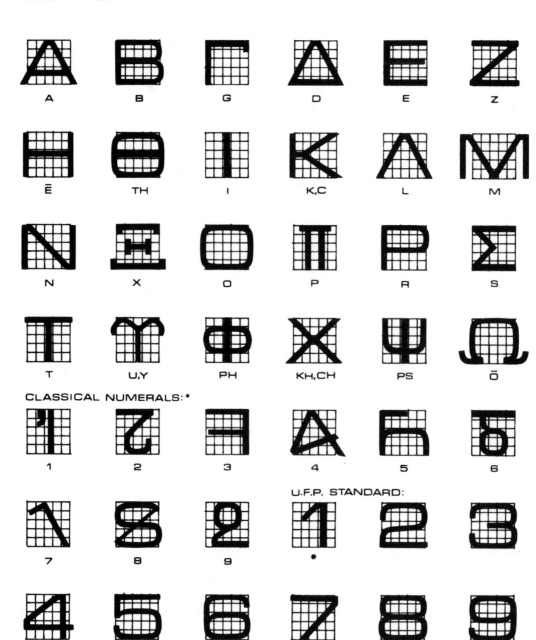

| | | | | | |
|---|---|---|---|---|---|
| A | B | G | D | E | Z |
| Ē | TH | I | K,C | L | M |
| N | X | O | P | R | S |
| T | U,Y | PH | KH,CH | PS | Ō |

CLASSICAL NUMERALS:*

| | | | | | |
|---|---|---|---|---|---|
| 1 | 2 | 3 | 4 | 5 | 6 |

U.F.P. STANDARD:

| | | | | | |
|---|---|---|---|---|---|
| 7 | 8 | 9 | * | 2 | 3 |
| 4 | 5 | 6 | 7 | 8 | 9 |

TYPICAL SPACING: ⊢2W  ONE UNIT ~H

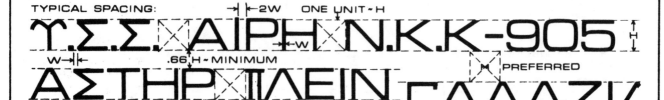

ϒ.Σ.Σ. ΑΙΡΗ N.K.K-905
.66 H ~MINIMUM
ΑΣΤΗΡ ΠΛΕΙΝ ΓΑΛΑΖΙΑ
PREFERRED

COMMON ALPHA KENTAURUS LANGUAGE FORM.  TYPE FONT: **Microgramma Ext.**

*DO NOT USE IN FLEET OPERATIONS, INSTRUMENTATION, OR SHIP DESIGNATIONS.

# UNIFORM COLOR CODE
## STAR FLEET SPECIFICATION

**01**
SILVER

**02**
ANTIMONY

**03**
GOLD

**04**
BRONZE

**05**
COPPER

**06**
WHITE

**07**
IVORY

**08**
SAND

**09**
BLOOD

**10**
RED

**11**
ORANGE

**12**
YELLOW

**13**
TENNE

**14**
OLIVE

**15**
GREEN

**16**
SKY BLUE

**17**
ULTRAMARINE

**18**
BLUE

**19**
INDIGO

**20**
MIDNIGHT

**21**
VIOLET

**22**
CORN

**23**
TAN

**24**
BROWN

**25**
NUDE

**26**
PURPLE

**27**
OXIDE

**28**
TAUPE

**29**
PLATINUM

**30**
GRAY

**31**
BLUEGRAY

**32**
BLACK

# COMMAND SECTION

| TO. NO: | SUBJECT | CURRENT | REPLACES |
|---|---|---|---|
| | SECTION INDEX | | |
| 01:00:05 | SECTION INDEX | 7309.10 | |
| » :04:22 | CLASS I TRANSP. CONT. - MK-IV DECK PLANS | 7306.03 | |
| | | | |
| » » :24 | CLASS I DREADNOUGHT - MK-X | 7306.09 | |
| » » :25 | AUTH. CONST. | 7306.15 | |
| | | | |
| » » :80 | SHUTTLECRAFT - 7 PERS. - MK-12B - EXTERNAL ARR. | 7502.20 | |
| » » :81 | »       »       »   »   »   » - INTERNAL ARR. | 7502.20 | |
| | | | |
| » :05:82 | TYP. SINGLE STATEROOM - PRIMARY HULL - CLASS I SS | 7312.21 | |
| » » :83 | »   DOUBLE   »   -   »   »   -   »   »   » | 7312.21 | |
| | | | |
| » :06:10 | MAIN BRIDGE - PRIMARY HULL - CLASS I SS - DECK I PLAN | 7409.07 | |
| » » :11 | »   »   »   »   »   »   » - ELEVATIONS | 7409.09 | |
| » » :12 | COMMAND MODULE - MAIN BRIDGE - PLAN & PROFILE | 7408.26 | |
| » » :13 | »   »   »   -   »   » - ELEVATIONS | 7408.26 | |
| » » :14 | MAIN BRIDGE - PRI. HULL - HELMSMAN'S STATION | 7409.02 | |
| » » :15 | »   »   -   »   » - NAVIGATOR'S   » | 7409.02 | |
| » » :16 | »   »   -   »   » - COMMAND CON | 7409.04 | |
| » » :17 | »   »   -   »   » - ASTROGATOR | 7409.05 | |
| | | | |
| » :07:20 | SECURITY SECTION - PRIMARY HULL - CLASS I SS | 7312.21 | |
| | | | |
| » :08:00 | DEFENSE & WEAPONS STATION - MAIN BRIDGE | * | |
| » » :01 | CONTROLS CONSOLE | * | |
| | | | |
| » » :50 | HAND PHASER - TYPE I - GENERAL ARRANGEMENT | 7304.16 | |
| | | | |
| » » :52 | HAND PHASER - TYPE II - GEN. ARR. | 7304.30 | |
| » » :53 | »   »   »   » - DETAILS | 7304.30 | |
| | | | |
| » » :58 | OFFENSIVE / DEFENSIVE RAY GUN - GEN. ARR. | 7503.22 | |

NOTE (*): NO CURRENT PRINT-OUT FROM MASTERCOM DATABANKS/SFHQ

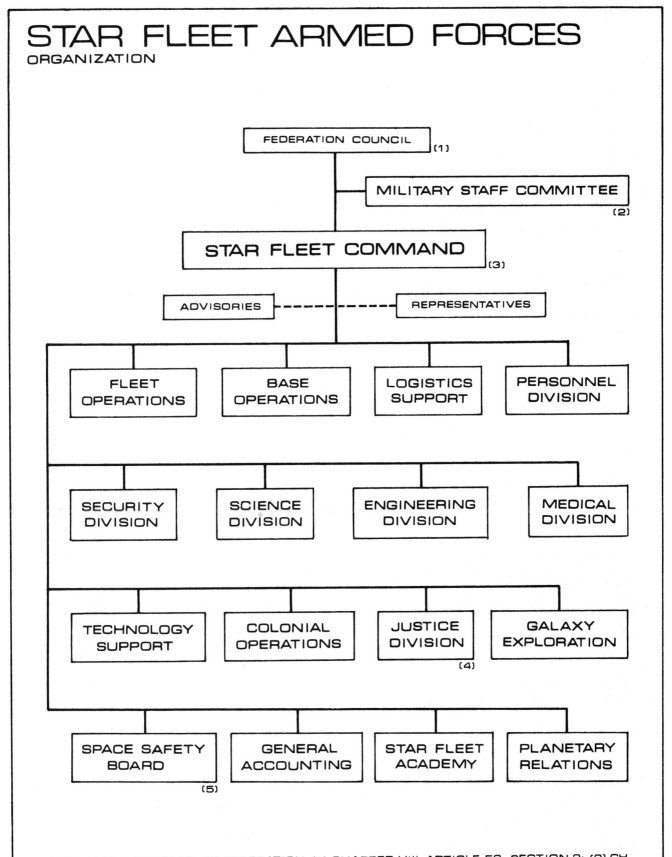

# STAR FLEET ARMED FORCES
ORGANIZATION

FEDERATION COUNCIL (1)

MILITARY STAFF COMMITTEE (2)

## STAR FLEET COMMAND (3)

ADVISORIES - - - - - - - REPRESENTATIVES

FLEET OPERATIONS

BASE OPERATIONS

LOGISTICS SUPPORT

PERSONNEL DIVISION

SECURITY DIVISION

SCIENCE DIVISION

ENGINEERING DIVISION

MEDICAL DIVISION

TECHNOLOGY SUPPORT

COLONIAL OPERATIONS

JUSTICE DIVISION (4)

GALAXY EXPLORATION

SPACE SAFETY BOARD (5)

GENERAL ACCOUNTING

STAR FLEET ACADEMY

PLANETARY RELATIONS

AUTHORITY: ARTICLES OF FEDERATION: (1) CHAPTER VIII, ARTICLE 52, SECTION 2; (2) CH. VIII, ART. 52, SECT. 2; (3) CH. VIII; (4) SUPREME COURT STATUTE, CH. II, ART. 15, SECT. 2; (5) INTERPLANETARY COMMERCE STATUTE, PART VIII, SECT. 47, ITEM 01.

# STAR FLEET ARMED FORCES
ORGANIZATION

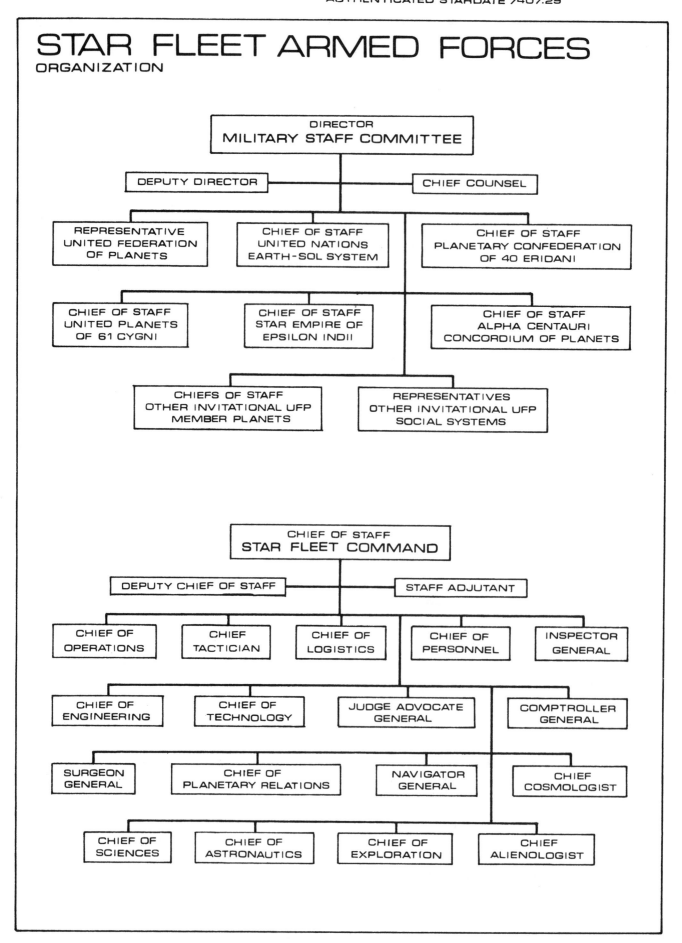

# STAR FLEET ARMED FORCES
ORGANIZATION

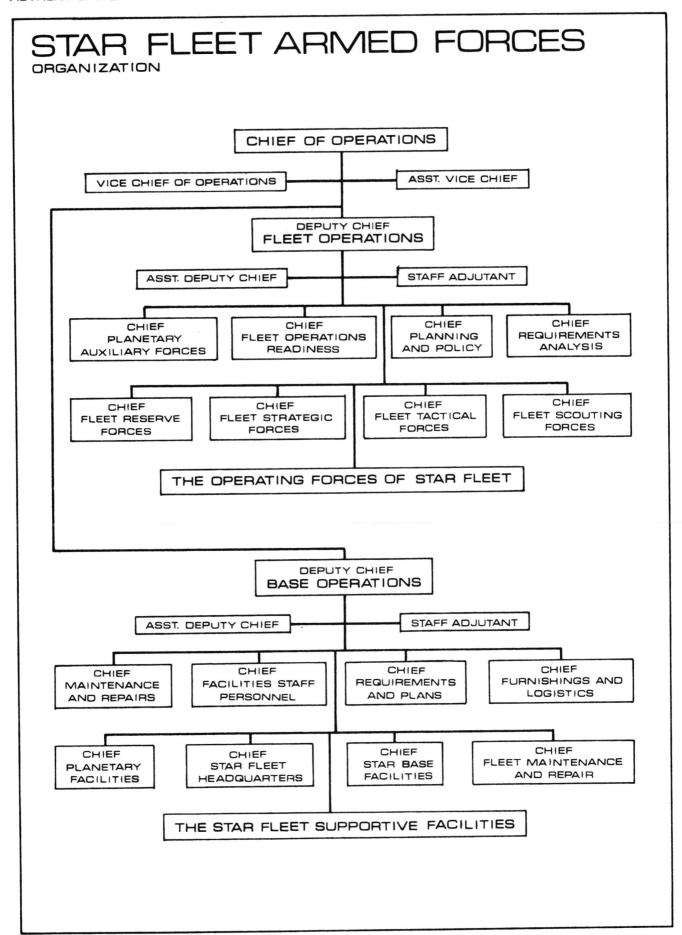

# STAR FLEET ARMED FORCES
ORGANIZATION

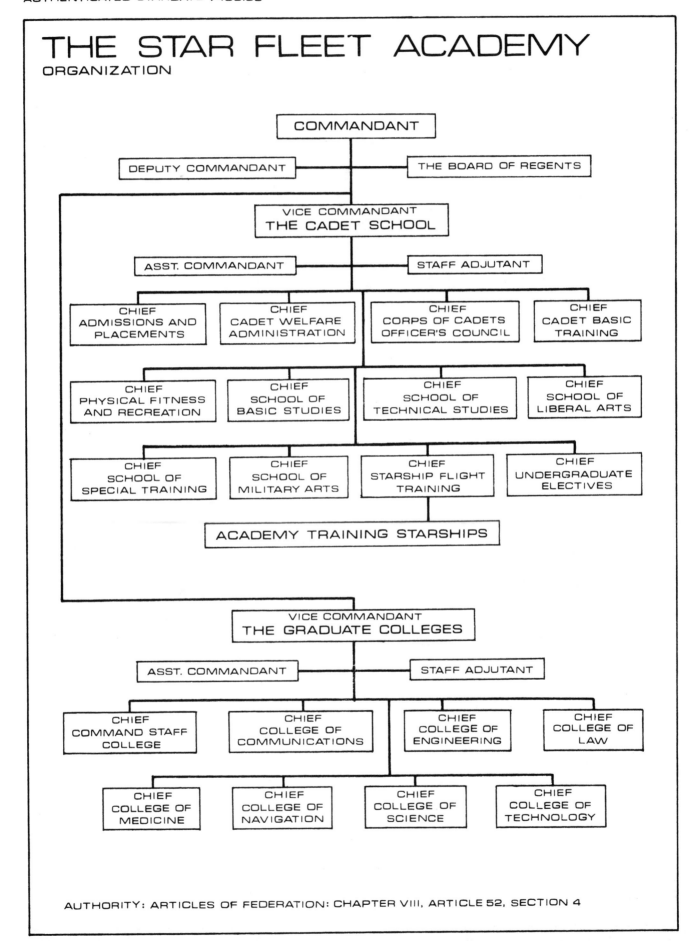

# THE STAR FLEET ACADEMY
ORGANIZATION

COMMANDANT

DEPUTY COMMANDANT — THE BOARD OF REGENTS

VICE COMMANDANT
THE CADET SCHOOL

ASST. COMMANDANT — STAFF ADJUTANT

CHIEF ADMISSIONS AND PLACEMENTS

CHIEF CADET WELFARE ADMINISTRATION

CHIEF CORPS OF CADETS OFFICER'S COUNCIL

CHIEF CADET BASIC TRAINING

CHIEF PHYSICAL FITNESS AND RECREATION

CHIEF SCHOOL OF BASIC STUDIES

CHIEF SCHOOL OF TECHNICAL STUDIES

CHIEF SCHOOL OF LIBERAL ARTS

CHIEF SCHOOL OF SPECIAL TRAINING

CHIEF SCHOOL OF MILITARY ARTS

CHIEF STARSHIP FLIGHT TRAINING

CHIEF UNDERGRADUATE ELECTIVES

ACADEMY TRAINING STARSHIPS

VICE COMMANDANT
THE GRADUATE COLLEGES

ASST. COMMANDANT — STAFF ADJUTANT

CHIEF COMMAND STAFF COLLEGE

CHIEF COLLEGE OF COMMUNICATIONS

CHIEF COLLEGE OF ENGINEERING

CHIEF COLLEGE OF LAW

CHIEF COLLEGE OF MEDICINE

CHIEF COLLEGE OF NAVIGATION

CHIEF COLLEGE OF SCIENCE

CHIEF COLLEGE OF TECHNOLOGY

AUTHORITY: ARTICLES OF FEDERATION: CHAPTER VIII, ARTICLE 52, SECTION 4

# FLEET HEADQUARTERS
## GENERAL ARRANGEMENT

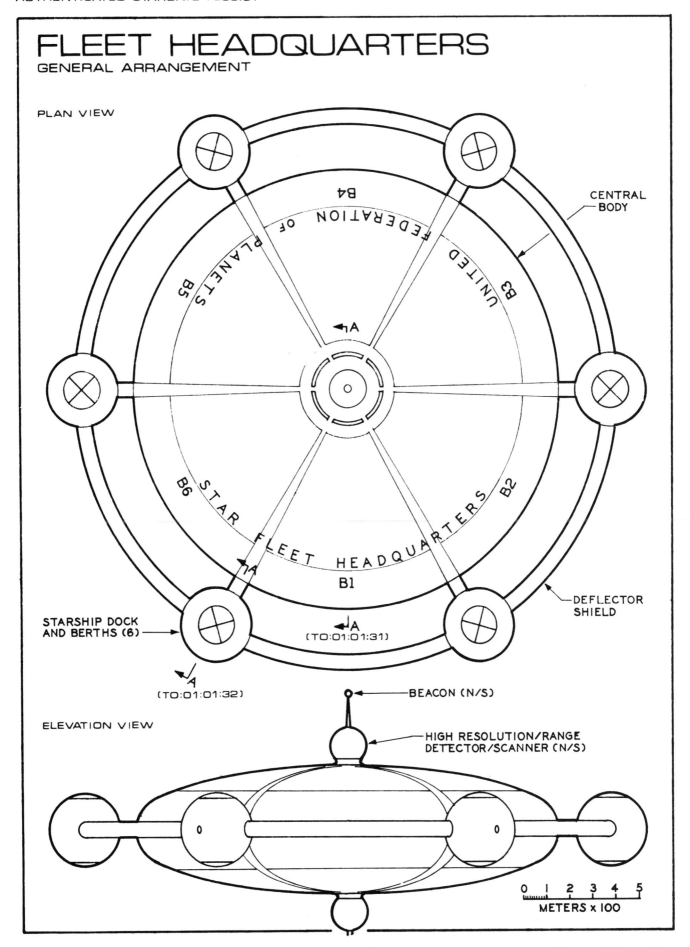

PLAN VIEW

CENTRAL BODY

B4

UNITED FEDERATION OF PLANETS

B3

B5

↤A

B6 STAR FLEET HEADQUARTERS B2

↤A

B1

DEFLECTOR SHIELD

STARSHIP DOCK AND BERTHS (6)

↙A
(TO:01:01:31)

↙A
(TO:01:01:32)

BEACON (N/S)

ELEVATION VIEW

HIGH RESOLUTION/RANGE DETECTOR/SCANNER (N/S)

0 1 2 3 4 5
METERS x 100

# FLEET HEADQUARTERS
## VIEW A-A TYPICAL CROSS-SECTION

CENTRAL POWER CORE

¢
B → (TO:01:01:33)

SUPPORTING STRUCTURE

TRITITANIUM TOROIDAL INNER SHELL

IONIZED FLOURESCENT GAS AT .84 KG.CM²

TRANSLUCENT FLOURESCENT INNER "SKY" SHELL

"SKY"
STD. AIR COMPOSITION
GAS AT 1.04 KG.CM²

STAR FLEET HEAD-QUARTERS BUILDING (DIV. BETWEEN BAYS)

(TO:01:01:34)  C↓

C↓

BAY-TO-BAY UNDERPASS (CENTER)

NATURAL HABITAT

"GROUND LEVEL"

SOIL LAYER

MANUFACTURING SHOPS, LABORATORIES, ETC.

TRANSPORTATION CORRIDORS (CENTER)

LAMINATED TRITITANIUM AND RODINIUN OUTER HULL SHELL

WAREHOUSE STORAGE

0 2 4 6 8 10
METERS x 10

B →

# FLEET HEADQUARTERS
## VIEW A-A TYPICAL DOCK CROSS-SECTION

NOTE:
DOCK IS NORMALLY PRESSURIZED
ONLY FOR EXTENSIVE EXTERNAL
SHIP REPAIRS OR LARGE SCALE
LOADING AND UNLOADING OPERA-
TIONS. SHIPS "FLOAT" IN
SYNCHRONOUS ORBIT
WITHIN DOCK

ELEVATORS

VIEW α-α

TURBO-LIFT
ELEVATOR
E/W

DESTROYER/SCOUT
CLASS STARSHIP

PRESSURE
SEAL

OBSERVATION/WORK GALLERY

NCC-585

DOOR JACK

WORK CRANE

DOOR QUADRANT

NCC-1700

TRACTOR
BEAM
N/S

ANTI-DRIFT
LINES

CRUISER CLASS
STARSHIP

STAR FLEET TRANSPORT C
NCC-4001

NCC-3801

CARGO CONTAINER

TRANSPORT-TUG
CLASS STARSHIP

SUPER PHASER TURRET

0  10 20 30 40 50

METERS

# FLEET HEADQUARTERS
## VIEW B-B TYPICAL EQUITORIAL SECTION

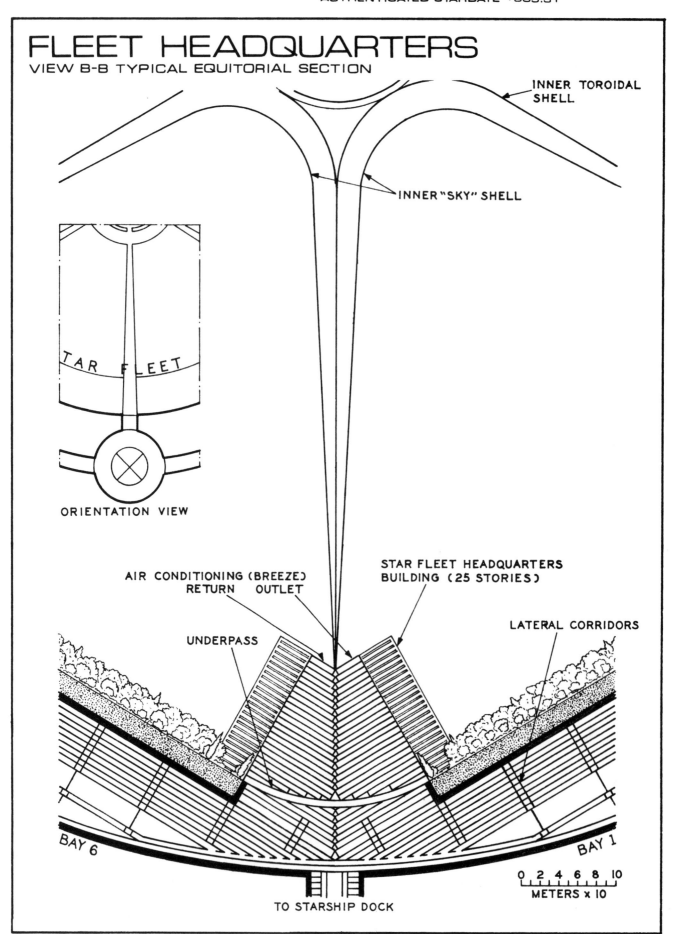

INNER TOROIDAL SHELL

INNER "SKY" SHELL

ORIENTATION VIEW

AIR CONDITIONING (BREEZE) RETURN OUTLET

STAR FLEET HEADQUARTERS BUILDING (25 STORIES)

LATERAL CORRIDORS

UNDERPASS

BAY 6

BAY 1

0 2 4 6 8 10
METERS x 10

TO STARSHIP DOCK

# FLEET HEADQUARTERS
## VIEW C-C GROUND LEVEL PLANS

SURFACE AREA EACH BAY 22.10 HECTARES

STAR FLEET HEADQUARTERS

CENTER CITY COMPLEX

B A Z A A R

BOAT DOCKS

BEACH

UNITED FEDERATION PARK

ERIDANUS LAGOON

CENTAURUS

RECREATION

STAR FLEET HISTORICAL MUSEUM

ALIEN CULTURE MUSEUM

AREA

APT

POOL

LAWN

TREES

TREES

TREES

R E S I D E N T I A L

CENTER CITY COMPLEX
SHOPS STORES OFFICES
HOTEL OVER

A P A R T M E N T S

BAY 1

0 2 4 6 8 10
METERS x 10

BAY 2

# FLEET HEADQUARTERS
## VIEW C-C GROUND LEVEL PLANS

RESIDENTIAL

APARTMENTS

SINGLE — FAMILY — RESIDENCES

PLAY

GROUND

TREES

CYGNUS LAGOON

ORION PARK

AMUSEMENT CENTER

BAY 3

AMUSEMENT CENTER

TWIN          PEAKS

CHURCH

ORCHARD

SCENIC   RURAL   PRODUCTIVE

CROP   FARMING

ORCHARD TREES

POND

BAY 4

0 2 4 6 8 10
METERS x 10

# FLEET HEADQUARTERS
## VIEW C-C GROUND LEVEL PLANS

HIDDEN CAVES

INDUS HILLS

STAR FLEET ACADEMY

WILDERNESS

SADR-POND

L A W N

RECREATION

CADET

PARADE

AREA

GROUND

SWIMMING POOL

POOL

UNITED NATIONS

FOOTBALL FIELD

PARK

TREES

TREES

ATHLETIC FIELD

STAR FLEET ACADEMY

STAR FLEET HEADQUARTERS

BAY 5

BAY 6

0 2 4 6 8 10
METERS x 10

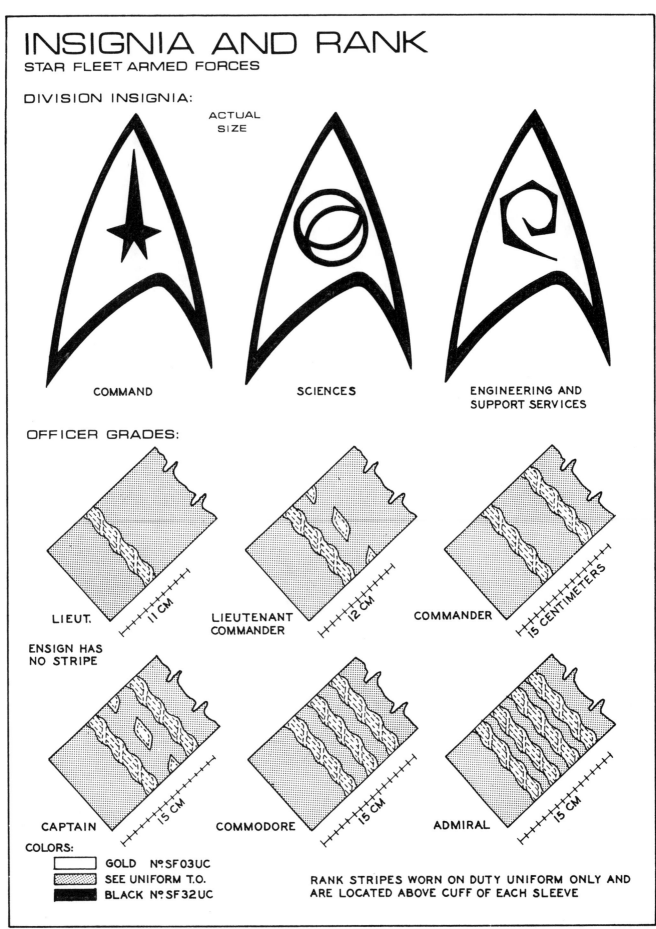

# INSIGNIA AND RANK
## STAR FLEET ARMED FORCES

DIVISION INSIGNIA:

ACTUAL SIZE

COMMAND

SCIENCES

ENGINEERING AND SUPPORT SERVICES

OFFICER GRADES:

LIEUT.                    11 CM

LIEUTENANT COMMANDER      12 CM

COMMANDER                 15 CENTIMETERS

ENSIGN HAS NO STRIPE

CAPTAIN      15 CM

COMMODORE    15 CM

ADMIRAL      15 CM

COLORS:

GOLD    N° SF03UC
SEE UNIFORM T.O.
BLACK   N° SF32UC

RANK STRIPES WORN ON DUTY UNIFORM ONLY AND
ARE LOCATED ABOVE CUFF OF EACH SLEEVE

# DUTY UNIFORM-MALE
## STAR FLEET ARMED FORCES

NECKBAND

6.4 CM

D.I.

9.2 CM

TUNIC

P  C

11.0 CM

1.5 CM

SERVICE
TROUSERS

9.2 CM
CUFF

34.3 CM HIGH
SERVICE BOOTS

30.2 CM
FROM
DECK

ENSIGN GRADE
SHOWN

COLORS:
DIV: COMMAND:         TENNE N°SF13UC          BLACK N°SF32UC
    SCIENCES:         BLUE  N°SF17UC    C-COMMUNICATOR, P-PHASER (UNDER TUNIC)
    ENGRG/OTHER:      RED   N°SF1OUC    D.I.-DIVISION INSIGNIA (SEE TO:01:03:00)

# UNIFORM PATTERN
## MALE - NON-COMPUTERIZED FABRICATION

RATIO UNIT UP OR DOWN FOR LARGER OR SMALLER SIZES. CUT TWO TOGETHER OF EACH GUSSET AND SLEEVE PATTERN. MAKE COLLAR FROM 13 x 44 CM BLACK RIBBING. PATTERN FOR USE WITH REGULATION STRETCH FABRICS ONLY. TROUSERS ARE REGULATION PATTERN WITHOUT POCKETS OR BELT - USE FITTED WAISTBAND. A - LENGTHEN OR SHORTEN PATTERN HERE. B, F - PLACE CENTERLINE ON FOLD OF FABRIC. C - CUFF FOR LONG ARM LENGTH. H - APPROXIMATE HEM LINE. N - NECK LINE. S - SEAM WIDTH ---- 1.60 CM. Z - INVISIBLE ZIPPER IN SEAM W/ TALON UP - IT MUST INCLUDE COLLAR. ADJUST PATTERN AT SEAMS FOR SMOOTH FIT.

# DUTY UNIFORM-FEMALE
## STAR FLEET ARMED FORCES

COLLAR

D.I.

MEDICAL DIV.
ONLY COLLAR
COLOR

TUNIC

5.1CM

7.6 CM

PANTYHOSE

34.3 CM HIGH
SERVICE BOOTS

OFFICER
GRADES
EXCEPT
ENSIGN

**COLORS:**
DIV: COMMAND          TENNE  N⁰SF13UC          NUDE  N⁰SF25UC
SCIENCES          BLUE  N⁰SF17UC          BLACK  N⁰SF32UC
ENGRG/OTHER          RED  N⁰SF10UC          D.I.- DIVISION INSIGNIA (SEE TO:01:03:00)

# OFF. UNIFORM PATTERN
## FEMALE - FOR NON-COMPUTERIZED FABRICATION

**RATIO UNIT UP OR DOWN FOR LARGER OR SMALLER SIZES. MAKE COLLAR FROM 13 X 74 CM BLACK RIBBING. B-WAISTBAND WIDTH-2 CM. C-CUFF. F-FLAP. H-HEM. S-SEAM WIDTH------1.60 CM. UF-UNDER FLAP. Z-INVISIBLE ZIPPER IN SEAM W/TALON UP. ADJUST SEAMS FOR SMOOTH FIT AND FLAP LENGTH FOR FLAT HANG. USE ELASTIC IN PANTY WAISTBAND AND LEG BANDS.**

# DUTY UNIFORM-FEMALE
## STAR FLEET ARMED FORCES

COLLAR

D.I.

TUNIC

5.1 CM

7.6 CM

PANTYHOSE

34.3 CM HIGH
SERVICE BOOTS

ENSIGN
GRADE
EXCEPT
MEDICAL

COLORS:

| DIV: | | | | |
|---|---|---|---|---|
| COMMAND........ | ☐ | TENNE | № SF13UC | |
| SCIENCES........ | ☐ | BLUE | № SF17UC | |
| ENGRG/OTHER... | ☐ | RED | № SF10UC | |

NUDE   № SF25UC
BLACK  № SF32UC
D.I.—DIVISION INSIGNIA (SEE TO:01:03:00)

# ENS. UNIFORM PATTERN
## FEMALE -NON-COMPUTERIZED FABRICATION

L. H. BACK TOP

R. H. BACK

UF

Z

D

MEDIAN SIZE 12 SHOWN

G

D

C

F

L. H. BACK BOTTOM

H

H

G

Z

L. H. BACK MIDDLE

C

C

R. H. FRONT TOP

S

EACH UNIT

16 SQ. CM

A

A

D

L. H. FRONT

A

E

C

R. H. FRONT MID.

E

Z

PANTY BACK

B

UF

B

PANTY FRONT

R. H. FRONT BOTTOM

H

F

H

H

LENGTH IN CENTIMETERS

RATIO UNIT UP OR DOWN FOR LARGER OR SMALLER SIZES. MAKE COLLAR FROM 13 x 80 CM BLACK RIBBING. B - WAISTBAND WIDTH - 2 CM. C - CUFF. F - FLAP. H - HEM. S - SEAM WIDTH --- 1.6 CM. UF - UNDER FLAP. Z - INVISIBLE ZIPPER IN SEAM W/TALON UP. ADJUST SEAMS FOR SMOOTH FIT AND FLAP LENGTH FOR FLAT HANG. USE ELASTIC IN PANTY WAISTBAND AND LEG BANDS.

# DUTY UNIFORM-FEMALE
## STAR FLEET ARMED FORCES

MEDICAL ENSIGN

COLLAR

D.I.

TUNIC

5.1 CM

7.6 CM

PANTYHOSE

34.3 CM HIGH
SERVICE BOOTS

**COLORS:**
DIV: SCIENCES

| | | |
|---|---|---|
| ☐ | BLUE | NºSF17UC |
| ▒ | NUDE | NºSF25UC |
| ■ | BLACK | NºSF32UC |

D.I. – DIVISION INSIGNIA FOR MEDICAL NURSES
AND ORDERLIES (SEE TO:01:03:01)

# MED. UNIFORM PATTERN
## FEMALE - NON-COMPUTERIZED FABRICATION

MEDIAN SIZE 12 SHOWN

L. H. BACK BOT. -R-

L. H. BACK BOT. -L-

R. H. BACK

L. H. COLLAR

PANTY FRONT

L. H. BACK MIDDLE

R. H. FRONT TOP

L. HAND BACK TOP

EACH UNIT

16 SQ. CM

L. H. FRONT

R. H. FRONT MID.

R. H. COLLAR

PANTY BACK

R. H. FRONT BOTTOM -L-

R. H. FRONT BOTTOM -R-

LENGTH IN CENTIMETERS

RATIO UNIT UP OR DOWN FOR LARGER OR SMALLER SIZES.   FOR INSTRUCTIONS SEE TO:01:03:15

# FLEET SHIP CLASSIFICATIONS
## CLASS I STARSHIPS

### DREADNOUGHT CLASS

MODEL: MK X
PROP: IMPULSE POWER
    3 SPACE/WARP UNITS
D.W.T: 285,000

UNDER CONSTRUCTION

### HEAVY CRUISER CLASS

NCC-1700

MOD: MK IX
PROP: IMP. PWR.
    2 S/W UNITS
D.W.T: 190,000

### DESTROYER/SCOUT CLASS

#### SCOUT CLASS
MOD: MK VII
PROP: IMPULSE POWER
    I S/W UNIT
D.W.T: 94,500

MOD: MK VIII
PROP: IMP. PWR.
    I S/W UNIT
D.W.T: 95,000

NCC-585

### TRANSPORT/TUG CLASS

TRANSPORT
CONTAINERS:
- MK V PRODUCTS
- MK IV PERSONNEL
- MK III REFERS
- MK II DRY BULK
- MK I BULK LIQUIDS

#### TUG:
MOD: MK VI
PROP: IMP. P.
    2 S/W U.
D.W.T: 126,500

NCC-3801

COMMAND
NCC-4000

(*)

NOTE: D.W.T.~ DEADWEIGHT METRIC TONNAGE; PROP.~ PROPULSION
    (*) TWO IN TANDEM STANDARD MAXIMUM

0 10 20 30 40 50
METERS

# CLASS I HEAVY CRUISER
## CONSTITUTION CLASS STARSHIPS

PHASER BANK P/S

IMPULSE POWER

SPACE/WARP PROPULSION 2 UNITS

PRIMARY HULL

BRIDGE

SENSOR ARRAY T/B

MAIN SENSOR

SHUTTLECRAFT HANGAR

SECONDARY HULL

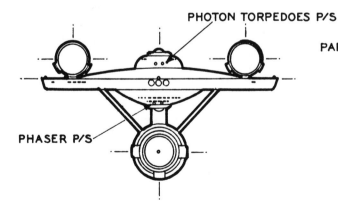

PHOTON TORPEDOES P/S

PHASER P/S

**PARTICULARS:**

| | |
|---|---|
| DEADWEIGHT TONNAGE-METRIC | 190,000 |
| STD. RANGE | 18 YEARS AT L.Y.V. |
| MAX. SAFE CRUISING SPEED | W/F 6 |
| EMERGENCY SPEED | W/F 8 |
| MAIN PHASERS | 3 BANKS/2 EACH |
| PHOTON TORPEDOES | 2 BANKS |
| LENGTH OVERALL-METERS | 288.6 |
| BREADTH OVERALL-METERS | 127.1 |
| HEIGHT OVERALL-METERS | 72.6 |
| PRIMARY HULL DIA.-METERS | 127.1 |
| SEC. HULL LENGTH-METERS | 103.6 |
| SEC. HULL MAX. DIA.-METERS | 34.1 |
| PROP. UNIT L.O.A.-METERS | 153.6 |
| PROP. UNIT DIA.-METERS | 17.3 |

**STD. SHIP'S COMPLEMENT:**

| | |
|---|---|
| OFFICERS (COMMAND) | 43 |
| CREW (ENSIGN GRADE) | 387 |

0 10 20 30 40 50

METERS

SEE BOOKLET OF GENERAL PLANS FOR DETAILS

# HEAVY CRUISER CLASS
## AUTHORIZED CONSTRUCTION

THE FOLLOWING SHIPS OF THE MK-IX CLASS WERE AUTHORIZED BY THE ORIGINAL ARTICLES OF FEDERATION OF STARDATE 0965:

| | | |
|---|---|---|
| CONSTELLATION – NCC-1017** | FARRAGUT – NCC-1702** | POTEMPKIN – NCC-1711 |
| CONSTITUTION – NCC-1700* | HOOD – NCC-1707 | REPUBLIC – NCC-1371 |
| ENTERPRISE – NCC-1701 | INTREPID – NCC-1708** | VALIANT – NCC-1709** |
| EXCALIBUR – NCC-1705 | KONGO – NCC-1710 | YORKTOWN – NCC-1704 |
| EXETER – NCC-1706 | LEXINGTON – NCC-1703 | |

THE FOLLOWING SHIPS OF THE MK-IXA CLASS WERE AUTHORIZED BY THE STAR FLEET APPROPRIATION OF STARDATE 3220:

| | | |
|---|---|---|
| ARI – NCC-1723 | EXCELSIOR – NCC-1718 | MONITOR – NCC-1713 |
| BONHOMME RICHARD – NCC-1712* | HORNET – NCC-1714 | SARATOGA – NCC-1724 |
| EAGLE – NCC-1719 | LAFAYETTE – NCC-1720 | TORI – NCC-1725 |
| EL DORADO – NCC-1722 | KRIEGER – NCC-1726 | WASP – NCC-1721 |
| ENDEAVOR – NCC-1716 | MERRIMAC – NCC-1715 | DEFIANCE – NCC-1717 |
| ESSEX – NCC-1727 | | |

THE FOLLOWING REPLACEMENTS FOR THE CONSTITUTION CLASS WERE AUTHORIZED BY STAR FLEET APPROPRIATION OF STARDATE 4444:

| | |
|---|---|
| CONSTELLATION II – NCC-1728 | INTREPID II – NCC-1730 |
| FARRAGUT II – NCC-1729 | VALIANT II – NCC-1731 |

THE FOLLOWING SHIPS OF THE MK-IXB CLASS WERE AUTHORIZED BY THE STAR FLEET APPROPRIATION OF STARDATE 5930:

| | | |
|---|---|---|
| ACHERNAR – NCC-1732* | FOMALHAUT – NCC-1804 | PILAR – NCC-1746 |
| ACRUX – NCC-1818 | GALINA – NCC-1764 | POLARIS – NCC-1839 |
| ADHARA – NCC-1827 | GHAR – NCC-1786 | POLLUX – NCC-1808 |
| AGENA – NCC-1816 | GHONDR – NCC-1749 | PROCYON – NCC-1756 |
| AHZDAR – NCC-1790 | HAJJ – NCC-1782 | PROXIMA – NCC-1737 |
| ALAM'AK – NCC-1796 | HELIOS – NCC-1825 | QUAL'AT – NCC-1776 |
| ALDEBARAN – NCC-1812 | HIEMDAL – NCC-1793 | QIZAN – NCC-1775 |
| ALFERAZ – NCC-1781 | HOR – NCC-1813 | QUINDAR – NCC-1736 |
| ALFR – NCC-1741 | HOROK – NCC-1748 | REGULUS – NCC-1840 |
| ALIOTH – NCC-1828 | JASSAN – NCC-1754 | RIGEL – NCC-1824 |
| ALKAID – NCC-1829 | JENSHAHN – NCC-1791 | RIGIL KENTAURUS – NCC-1735 |
| ALNILAM – NCC-1830 | JUPITER – NCC-1734 | SALAYNA – NCC-1774 |
| ALTAIR – NCC-1803 | KARS – NCC-1769 | SAMAARA – NCC-1765 |
| ANAK – NCC-1821 | KASIMAR – NCC-1784 | SARDAR – NCC-1811 |
| ANDROCUS – NCC-1738 | KEP SALU – NCC-1767 | SHAHR – NCC-1745 |
| ANNOBON – NCC-1752 | KESTRAL – NCC-1766 | SHAULA – NCC-1841 |
| ANTARES – NCC-1820 | KETOI – NCC-1768 | SHAANDRA – NCC-1795 |
| ARCTURUS – NCC-1807 | K'HOTAN – NCC-1802 | SINUIJI – NCC-1770 |
| ARIDED – NCC-1831 | K'USHUI – NCC-1801 | SIRIUS – NCC-1744 |
| ASTRAD – NCC-1739 | LUX – NCC-1823 | SOL – NCC-1733 |
| BEHR'AK – NCC-1797 | MIAPLACIDAS – NCC-1836 | SPICA – NCC-1815 |
| BELLATRIX – NCC-1832 | MAAT – NCC-1794 | TALI – NCC-1751 |
| BETELGEUSE – NCC-1822 | MAZDA – NCC-1778 | TAJARHI – NCC-1783 |
| BINAR – NCC-1819 | MENGEN – NCC-1773 | TEMIR – NCC-1763 |
| CANOPUS – NCC-1814 | MIRFAK – NCC-1837 | THELONII – NCC-1742 |
| CAPELLA – NCC-1809 | MIRAZH – NCC-1788 | THOLUS – NCC-1747 |
| CASPAN – NCC-1753 | MONDOLOY – NCC-1740 | TIKOPAI – NCC-1800* |
| CASTOR – NCC-1833 | MONGO – NCC-1785 | TULAN – NCC-1777 |
| CZAR'AK – NCC-1798 | MURZIM – NCC-1838 | TUTAKAI – NCC-1799 |
| DARION – NCC-1810 | NDELE – NCC-1758 | VEGA – NCC-1806 |
| DENEB – NCC-1826 | NAKARAT – NCC-1805 | VENA – NCC-1817 |
| DUBHE – NCC-1834 | OOMARU – NCC-1761 | WEZEN – NCC-1842 |
| EL NATH – NCC-1835 | OBLIK – NCC-1772 | XANTHII – NCC-1743 |
| ELOHIM – NCC-1792 | PARI – NCC-1787 | YAAN – NCC-1762 |
| EKINUS – NCC-1771 | PAEGAN – NCC-1755 | ZAAHM – NCC-1780 |
| ESABL – NCC-1779 | PELIONE – NCC-1750 | ZA'FARAN – NCC-1760 |
| ESKIIS – NCC-1789 | PHARDOS – NCC-1757 | ZINDAR – NCC-1759 |

*CLASS SHIP.  **LOST IN THE LINE OF DUTY.  ALL NAMES PRECEDED WITH "U.S.S."

# CLASS I DESTROYER
## SALADIN CLASS STARSHIPS

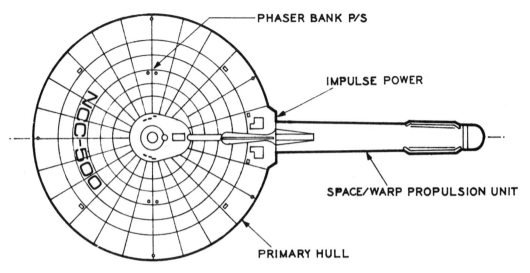

PHASER BANK P/S

IMPULSE POWER

SPACE/WARP PROPULSION UNIT

PRIMARY HULL

BRIDGE     SENSOR ARRAY

NCC-500

MAIN SENSOR

PHOTON TORPEDOS P/S

PHASER P/S

**PARTICULARS:**

| | |
|---|---|
| DEADWEIGHT TONNAGE-METRIC | 95,000 |
| STD. RANGE | 9 YEARS AT L.Y.V. |
| MAX. SAFE CRUISING SPEED | W/F 6 |
| EMERGENCY SPEED | W/F 8 |
| MAIN PHASERS | 3 BANKS/2 EACH |
| PHOTON TORPEDOES | 2 BANKS |
| LENGTH OVERALL-METERS | 242.5 |
| BREADTH OVERALL-METERS | 127.1 |
| HEIGHT OVERALL-METERS | 60 |
| PRIMARY HULL DIA.-METERS | 127.1 |
| PROP. UNIT L.O.A-METERS | 153.6 |
| PROP. UNIT DIA.-METERS | 17.3 |

0  10 20 30 40 50
METERS

**STD. SHIP'S COMPLEMENT:**

| | |
|---|---|
| OFFICERS (COMMAND) | 20 |
| CREW (ENSIGN GRADE) | 180 |

SEE BOOKLET OF GENERAL PLANS FOR DETAILS

# DESTROYER CLASS
## AUTHORIZED CONSTRUCTION

THE FOLLOWING SHIPS OF THE MK-VIII CLASS WERE AUTHORIZED BY THE ORIGINAL ARTICLES OF FEDERATION OF STARDATE 0965:

| | | |
|---|---|---|
| ADAD – NCC-515 | HAMILCAR – NCC-518 | SHAITAN – NCC-519 |
| AHRIMAN – NCC-513 | HANNIBAL – NCC-512 | SALADIN – NCC-500* |
| ALARIC – NCC-503 | HASHISHIYUN – NCC-516 | SARGON – NCC-504 |
| ALEXANDER – NCC-511 | JENGHIZ – NCC-501 | SULEIMAN – NCC-508 |
| AZRAEL – NCC-517 | KUBLAI – NCC-507 | TAMERLANE – NCC-510 |
| DARIUS – NCC-502 | POMPEY – NCC-506 | XERXES – NCC-505 |
| ETZEL – NCC-509 | RAHMAN – NCC-514 | |

THE FOLLOWING SHIPS OF THE MK-VIIIA CLASS WERE AUTHORIZED BY STAR FLEET APPROPRIATION OF STARDATE 3030:

| | | |
|---|---|---|
| ARES – NCC-524 | LOKI – NCC-529 | SIVA – NCC-520* |
| HATHOR – NCC-523 | LUCIFER – NCC-521 | TYR – NCC-526 |
| IBLIS – NCC-528 | MARS – NCC-525 | |
| JUGURTHA – NCC-527 | MOLOCK – NCC-522 | |

THE FOLLOWING SHIPS OF THE MK-VIIIB CLASS WERE AUTHORIZED BY STAR FLEET APPROPRIATION OF STARDATE 4699:

| | | |
|---|---|---|
| ABU BEKR – NCC-549 | COCHISE – NCC-530* | MARTEL – NCC-554 |
| ACHILLES – NCC-551 | CORTEZ – NCC-536 | NELSON – NCC-546 |
| AJAX – NCC-547 | DE RUYTER – NCC-538 | NEY – NCC-533 |
| AKBAR – NCC-548 | DRAKE – NCC-541 | PERSEUS – NCC-544 |
| ALVA – NCC-531 | EL CID – NCC-534 | PONTIAC – NCC-532 |
| ALVARADO – NCC-537 | GERONIMO – NCC-535 | SCIPIO – NCC-553 |
| AL MAHDI – NCC-545 | HEKTOR – NCC-539 | SAMSON – NCC-543 |
| APPOLLYON – NCC-542 | IVAN – NCC-550 | THESEUS – NCC-552 |
| CIMON – NCC-555 | LYSANDER – NCC-540 | |

*CLASS SHIP.  ALL NAMES PRECEDED WITH "U.S.S."

# CLASS I SCOUT
## HERMES CLASS STARSHIPS

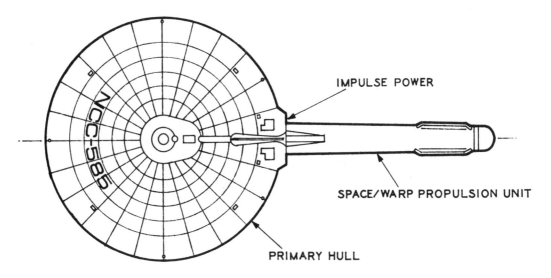

IMPULSE POWER

SPACE/WARP PROPULSION UNIT

PRIMARY HULL

BRIDGE — SENSOR ARRAY

MAIN SENSOR

NCC-585

PHASER P/S

**PARTICULARS:**

DEADWEIGHT TONNAGE-METRIC..........94,500
STD. RANGE........................9 YEARS AT L.Y.V.
MAX. SAFE CRUISING SPEED.................W/F 6
EMERGENCY SPEED................................W/F 8
MAIN PHASERS....................... I BANK/2 EACH
LENGTH OVERALL-METERS....................242.5
BREADTH OVERALL-METERS...................127.1
HEIGHT OVERALL-METERS..........................60
PRIMARY HULL DIA.-METERS.................127.1
PROP. UNIT L.O.A.-METERS.....................153.6
PROP. UNIT DIA.-METERS.......................17.3

**STD. SHIP'S COMPLEMENT:**

OFFICERS (COMMAND)..........................20
CREW (ENSIGN GRADE).....................175

0  10 20 30 40 50
METERS

SEE BOOKLET OF GENERAL PLANS FOR DETAILS

# SCOUT CLASS
## AUTHORIZED CONSTRUCTION

THE FOLLOWING SHIPS OF THE MK-VII CLASS WERE AUTHORIZED BY THE ORIGINAL
ARTICLES OF FEDERATION OF STARDATE 0965:

| | | |
|---|---|---|
| AEOLUS – NCC-588 | CARSON – NCC-592 | QUINTILLUS – NCC-590 |
| ANUBIS – NCC-586 | CODY – NCC-594 | REVERE – 595 |
| BATIDOR – NCC-593 | CROCKETT – NCC-600 | SACAJAWEA – NCC-598 |
| BOWIE – NCC-597 | DIANA – NCC-589 | SPAKER – 596 |
| BRIDGER – NCC-591 | HERMES – NCC-585* | TONTI – NCC-599 |

THE FOLLOWING SHIPS OF THE MK-VIIA CLASS WERE AUTHORIZED BY STAR FLEET
APPROPRIATION OF STARDATE 3669:

| | | |
|---|---|---|
| ARIES – NCC-602 | LEO MINOR – NCC-614 | PEGASUS – NCC-612 |
| CAMELOPARDUS – NCC-606 | LEPUS – NCC-610 | TAURUS – NCC-605 |
| CANIS MAJOR – NCC-611 | LUPUS – NCC-604 | URSA MAJOR – NCC-609 |
| CANIS MINOR – NCC-615 | LYNX – NCC-608 | URSA MINOR – NCC-616 |
| EQUULUS – NCC-603 | MONOCEROS – NCC-601* | VULPECULA – NCC-613 |
| LEO – NCC-607 | | |

THE FOLLOWING SHIPS OF THE MK-VIIB CLASS WERE AUTHORIZED BY STAR FLEET
APPROPRIATION OF STARDATE 5099. THEY ARE SPECIALLY OUTFITTED FOR REGULAR
DUTY AS COMMAND AND DIPLOMATIC COURRIERS:

| | | |
|---|---|---|
| APUS – NCC-618 | CORVUS – NCC-620 | PAVO – NCC-622 |
| AQUILA – NCC-623 | CYGNUS – NCC-617* | PHOENIX – NCC-625 |
| COLUMBIA – NCC-621 | GRUS – NCC-624 | TUCANA – NCC-619 |

*CLASS SHIP.   ALL NAMES PRECEDED WITH "U.S.S."

# CLASS I TRANSPORT/TUG
## PTOLEMY CLASS STARSHIPS

PHASER P/S

SPACE/WARP PROPULSION
2 UNITS

IMPULSE POWER

PRIMARY HULL

BRIDGE

SENSOR ARRAY

TOW PAD

NCC-3801

MAIN SENSOR

PHASER P/S

PARTICULARS:

DEADWEIGHT TONNAGE - METRIC........126,500
STD. RANGE....................9 YEARS AT L.Y.V.
MAX. SAFE CRUISING SPEED..............W/F 6
EMERGENCY SPEED.................................W/F 8
MAIN PHASERS...................2 BANKS/2 EACH
LENGTH OVERALL-METERS.......................222
BREADTH OVERALL-METERS..................127.1
HEIGHT OVERALL-METERS..........................66
PRIMARY HULL DIA.-METERS..................127.1
PROP. UNIT L.O.A.-METERS....................153.6
PROP. UNIT DIA.-METERS.....................17.3

0 10 20 30 40 50
METERS

STD. SHIP'S COMPLEMENT:
OFFICERS (COMMAND).................22
CREW (ENSIGN GRADE).................198

SEE BOOKLET OF GENERAL PLANS FOR DETAILS

# TRANSP./TUG CLASS
## AUTHORIZED CONSTRUCTION

THE FOLLOWING SHIPS OF THE MK-VI CLASS WERE AUTHORIZED BY THE ORIGINAL ARTICLES OF FEDERATION OF STARDATE 0965:

| | | |
|---|---|---|
| AL RASHID – NCC-3802 | ERATOSTHENES – NCC-3807 | PHILOLAUS – NCC-3811 |
| ANAXAGORAS – NCC-3803 | GALILEI – NCC-3808 | PTOLEMY – NCC-3801* |
| ANAXIMANDER – NCC-3804 | HEVELIUS – NCC-3814 | PYTHAGORAS – NCC-3812 |
| ARISTARCHUS – NCC-3805 | HIPPARCHUS – NCC-3809 | THALES – NCC-3813 |
| COPERNICUS – NCC-3815 | IBN DAUD – NCC-3806 | ULUGH BEG – NCC-3810 |

THE FOLLOWING SHIPS OF THE MK-VIA CLASS WERE AUTHORIZED BY STAR FLEET APPROPRIATION OF STARDATE 3640:

| | | |
|---|---|---|
| AMBARTSUMIAN – NCC-3817 | FLAMARION – NCC-3818 | LUYTEN – NCC-3829 |
| BRAHE – NCC-3821 | KEPPLER – NCC-3816 * | NEWTON – NCC-3822 |
| CASSINI – NCC-3824 | KIDINNU – NCC-3826 | PIAZZI – NCC-3827 |
| DESLANDRES – NCC-3820 | LEVERRIER – NCC-3828 | RICCIOLI – NCC-3823 |
| DONATI – NCC-3825 | MESSIER – NCC-3830 | SCHIAPARELLI – NCC-3819 |

THE FOLLOWING SHIPS OF THE MK-VIB CLASS WERE AUTHORIZED BY STAR FLEET APPROPRIATION OF STARDATE 4990:

| | | |
|---|---|---|
| ADAMS – NCC-3925 | HALE – NCC-3873 | PIERCE – NCC-3931 |
| AIRY – NCC-3842 | HALL – NCC-3926 | PICKERING – NCC-3864 |
| APIAN – NCC-3896 | HALLEY – NCC-3833 | POGSON – NCC-3906 |
| BAADE – NCC-3855 | HAYASHI – NCC-3887 | POPPER – NCC-3878 |
| BAUM – NCC-3935 | HENCKE – NCC-3847 | PLASKETT – NCC-3918 |
| BAYER – NCC-3869 | HENDERSON – NCC-3914 | PRITCHETT – NCC-3838 |
| BESSEL – NCC-3911 | HERSCHELL – NCC-3860 | REBER – NCC-3892 |
| BIELA – NCC-3884 | HERTZSPRUNG – NCC-3902 | RITTENHOUSE – NCC-3851 |
| BODE – NCC-3922 | HIRAYAMA – NCC-3874 | ROQUES – NCC-3932 |
| BONDI – NCC-3843 | HOYLE – NCC-3928 | ROSS – NCC-3865 |
| BROUWER – NCC-3897 | HOLDEN – NCC-3834 | RUSSELL – NCC-3907 |
| CAMPELL – NCC-3856 | HUBBARD – NCC-3888 | SABINE – NCC-3879 |
| CARPENTER – NCC-3936 | HUBBLE – NCC-3848 | SANDAGE – NCC-3919 |
| CARRINGTON – NCC-3870 | HUGGINS – NCC-3915 | SAVARY – NCC-3839 |
| CHALLIS – NCC-3912 | HUMANSON – NCC-3861 | SCHEINER – NCC-3893 |
| CHAMBERLAIN – NCC-3883 | IRWIN – NCC-3903 | SCHMIDT – NCC-3880 |
| CHANDRASEKHER – NCC-3923 | JANSKY – NCC-3875 | SECCHI – NCC-3852 |
| CHAUVENET – NCC-3844 | JEANS – NCC-3929 | SHAPLEY – NCC-3933 |
| CLARK – NCC-3898 | JEFFREY – NCC-3835 | SHKLOVSKY – NCC-3866 |
| COLUMBO – NCC-3857 | KAULA – NCC-3889 | SLIPHER – NCC-3908 |
| DELAMBRE – NCC-3937 | KLEPSTRA – NCC-3862 | SCHAWBE – NCC-3920 |
| DOLLFUS – NCC-3885 | KOHLSCHUTTER – NCC-3904 | STRUVE – NCC-3840 |
| DOLLOND – NCC-3900* | KRUGER – NCC-3871 | SWIFT – NCC-3894 |
| DOPPLER – NCC-3831* | KUIPER – NCC-3836 | TODD – NCC-3934 |
| DREYER – NCC-3899 | LAGRANGE – NCC-3916 | TOMBAUGH – NCC-3853 |
| EDDINGTON – NCC-3845 | LAPLACE – NCC-3876 | TOSCANELLI – NCC-3867 |
| EICHELBERGER – NCC-3924 | LEAVITT – NCC-3849 | VAN DE HULST – NCC-3909 |
| ENCKE – NCC-3859 | LANGLEY – NCC-3930 | VAN DE KAMP – NCC-3881 |
| FLAMSTEED – NCC-3913 | LOCKYER – NCC-3890 | VAN MAANEN – NCC-3940 |
| FRACASTOR – NCC-3872 | LOWELL – NCC-3939 | VOGEL – NCC-3841 |
| FROST – NCC-3938 | MITCHELL – NCC-3863 | VON ZACH – NCC-3882 |
| GAILLOT – NCC-3832 | MOULTON – NCC-3905 | WALKER – NCC-3895 |
| GALLE – NCC-3886 | NEWCOMB – NCC-3877 | WOLASTON – NCC-3854 |
| GAUTIER – NCC-3846 | OLBERS – NCC-3917 | WOLF – NCC-3921 |
| GOLD – NCC-3927 | OORT – NCC-3837 | WRIGHT – NCC-3868 |
| GOLDRICKE – NCC-3859 | PALITZSCH – NCC-3891 | YOUNG – NCC-3910 |
| GOLDREICH – NCC-3901 | PEALE – NCC-3850 | |

*CLASS SHIP.   ALL NAMES PRECEDED WITH "U.S.S."

# TRANSPORT CONTAINERS
## CLASS I STARSHIPS - USE WITH CLASS I TUG

### MK-V PRODUCTS:

D.W. TONNAGE - METRIC......121,566
GROSS VOL. - M³................303,916
GR. FLR. AREA - M²............76,280
UNIT LOADING................1.59 T/M²
VOL. LOADING.............364 KG/M³
TRANSPORTERS.........................6
ELEVATORS.............................4
LOAD HEIGHT - METERS..........2.44
LENGTH O.A. - METERS .........200
DIAMETER - METERS..................40

PLAN

STAR FLEET TRANSPORT COMMAND
NCC-5000

PROFILE

CORRIDORS

ELEVATORS

12 STORAGE DECKS

ENVIRONMENTAL MAINT. MACHINERY SPACE

TRANSPORTERS P/S

CROSS-SECTIONS

### MK-III REEFERS:
#### REFRIGERATED GOODS

D.W. TONNAGE - METRIC......100,000
GROSS VOL. - M................303,916
GR. FLR. AREA - M.............76,280
UNIT LOADING................1.18 T/M
VOL. LOADING.............182 KG/M
TRANSPORTERS.........................6
ELEVATORS.............................4
LOAD HEIGHT - METERS..........2.44
LENGTH O.A. - METERS ..........200
DIAMETER - METERS..............40

PLAN

STAR FLEET TRANSPORT COMMAND
NCC-3000

PROFILE

0 10 20 30 40 50
METERS

CORRIDORS

ELEVATORS

12 STORAGE DECKS

ENVIRONMENTAL MAINT. MACHINERY SPACE

TRANSPORTERS P/S

0 10 20 30 40 50
METERS

CROSS-SECTIONS

SEE BOOKLETS OF GENERAL PLANS FOR DETAILS

# TRANSPORT CONTAINERS
## CLASS I STARSHIPS-USE WITH CLASS I TUG

### MK-II DRY BULK:

| | |
|---|---|
| D.W. TONNAGE-METRIC | 121,566 |
| GROSS VOL.-M$^3$ | 303,916 |
| NET VOLUME-M$^3$ | 276,076 |
| UNIT LOADING | 30 T/M$^2$ |
| VOL. LOADING | 364 KG/M$^3$ |
| TRANSPORTERS | 6 |
| ELEVATORS | 2 |
| LENGTH O.A.-METERS | 200 |
| DIAMETER-METERS | 40 |

PLAN

STAR FLEET TRANSPORT COMMAND
NCC-2000

PROFILE

SERVICE DECK

ELEVATORS    18 LOAD BINS    17 DIVISION BULKHEADS

ENVIRONMENTAL MAINT. MACHINERY SPACE    TRANSPORTERS T/B

CROSS-SECTIONS

### MK-I LIQUIDS:

| | |
|---|---|
| D.W. TONNAGE-METRIC | 121,566 |
| GROSS VOL.-M$^3$ | 303,916 |
| NET VOLUME-M$^3$ | 276,076 |
| UNIT LOADING | 30 T/M$^2$ |
| VOL. LOADING | 364 KG/M$^3$ |
| TRANSPORTERS | 6 |
| ELEVATORS | 2 |
| LENGTH O.A.-METERS | 200 |
| DIAMETER-METERS | 40 |

PLAN

STAR FLEET TRANSPORT COMMAND
NCC-1000

PROFILE

0 10 20 30 40 50
METERS

SERVICE DECK

ELEVATORS    ANTI-SURGE BAFFLES
BHD    BHD    BHD    BHD    BHD

ENVIRONMENTAL MAINT. MACHINERY SPACE    TRANSPORTERS T/B

0 10 20 30 40 50
METERS

CROSS-SECTIONS

SEE BOOKLETS OF GENERAL PLANS FOR DETAILS

# TRANSPORT CONTAINER
## CLASS I STARLINERS - USE WITH CLASS I TUG

### MK-IV PEOPLE:

D.W. TONNAGE-METRIC........80,000
GROSS VOL.-M³................303,916
GR. FLR. AREA-M².............77,570
UNIT LOADING............488 KG/M²
DECK SPACING-METERS...............3
TRANSPORTERS...................6/2
ELEVATORS.......................5
L.O.A x DIA.-METERS........200 x 18
OFFICERS (COMMAND)..............15
CREW (ENSIGN GRADE)...........150
PASSENGERS.....................500

PLAN

STAR FLEET TRANSPORT COMMAND
NCC-4000

PROFILE

0 10 20 30 40 50
METERS

FWD. ELEVATORS    BRIDGE    PROMENADE    DECKS A-B-C-D-E-F-G-H

CARGO
TRANSPORTER P/S    SENSOR    1ST-2ND-3RD CARGO HOLDS    TANK TOP

CROSS-SECTIONS

0 10 20 30 40 50
METERS

## DECK PLANS

### A DECK

FOUNTAIN

REFRESH-
MENT
LOUNGE

ELEVATOR

ADM. OFFICERS    ELEVATORS    ELEVATORS    PARK PROMENADE

### B DECK

106
ROOMS
212
PEOPLE

OFFICERS — CREW-91 STATEROOMS —    REC. LOUNGE    SPCL. ACCOM

### C DECK

127
ROOMS
254
PEOPLE

PASSENGERS -127 STATEROOMS    REC. LOUNGE

NOTE: CONTAINER IS A SELF-CONTAINED EMERGENCY LIFEBOAT WITH SUB-LIGHT VELOCITY AND 18
YEARS ENDURANCE

# MK-IV STARLINER
## DECK PLANS

# MK-IV STARLINER
## DECK PLANS AND DETAILS

2ND CARGO HOLD — 40,000 M³ CAP.

SHIP'S COMPUTERS ELEVATORS ELEVATORS ELEVATOR

3RD CARGO HOLD — 24,000 M³ CAP.

REFRIGERATED GOODS WASTE RECONSTITUTION HYDROPONIC GARDENS

TANK TOP — 28,900 M³ CAP.

CARGO TRANSPORTER P/S SOLID FUEL P/S

FRESH WATER TANKS P/S BASIC ELEMENTS P/S

0 10 20 30 40 50
METERS

END VIEWS
FORWARD
AFT

TYPICAL ACCOMMODATIONS

PASSAGEWAY PASSAGEWAY
TL
TL

STATEROOM – 23 M² BATH – 4 M²

0 1 2 3
METERS

# CLASS I DREADNOUGHT
FEDERATION CLASS STARSHIPS

MK-X

PHASER BANK P/S

IMPULSE POWER

SPACE/WARP PROPULSION
3 UNITS

PRIMARY HULL

0 10 20 30 40 50
METERS

SENSOR ARRAYS T/B

NCC-2100

SHUTTLECRAFT HANGAR
MAIN SENSOR F/A

PHASER BANK T/B

SECONDARY HULL

PHOTON
TORPEDOES
P/S

PHASER
BANK

TRACTOR BEAM

NAVIGATIONAL
DEFLECTOR

PARTICULARS:

DEADWEIGHT TONNAGE-METRIC:........ 285,000
STD. RANGE:.................... 20 YEARS AT L.Y.V.
MAX. SAFE CRUISING SPEED:.................W/F 8
EMERGENCY SPEED:................................W/F 10
MAIN PHASERS:...............5 BANKS/2 EACH
PHOTON TORPEDOES.............................2 BANKS
LENGTH OVERALL-METERS:....................320
BREADTH OVERALL-METERS:.................140
HEIGHT OVERALL-METERS:................... 87
PRIMARY HULL DIA.-METERS:................140
SEC. HULL LENGTH-METERS:..................122
SEC. HULL MAX. DIA.-METERS:................30
PROP. UNIT L.O.A.-METERS:...................153.6
PROP. UNIT DIA.-METERS:......................17.3

STD. SHIP'S COMPLEMENT:
OFFICERS (COMMAND)....................... 55
CREW (ENSIGN GRADE)....................445

# DREADNOUGHT CLASS
## AUTHORIZED CONSTRUCTION

THE FOLLOWING SHIPS OF THE MK-X CLASS WERE AUTHORIZED BY STAR FLEET
APPROPRIATION OF STARDATE 6066:

| | | |
|---|---|---|
| AFFILIATION – NCC-2108 | CORPORATION – NCC-2104 | STAR EMPIRE – NCC-2116 |
| ALLIANCE – NCC-2113 | DIRECTORATE – NCC-2110 | STAR LEAGUE – NCC-2101 |
| ASSOCIATION – NCC-2118 | DOMINION – NCC-2115 | STAR SYSTEM – NCC-2107 |
| COMPACTAT – NCC-2103 | ENTENTE – NCC-2120 | STAR UNION – NCC-2112 |
| CONCORDAT – NCC-2109 | FEDERATION – NCC-2100 * | TRUSTEESHIP – NCC-2117 |
| CONFEDERATION – NCC-2114 | KONKORDIUM – NCC-2106 | UNIFICATUM – NCC-2102 |
| CONSORTIUM – NCC-2119 | ORGANIZATION – NCC-2111 | |

*CLASS SHIP.  ALL NAMES PRECEDED WITH "U.S.S."

# SHUTTLECRAFT
## 7 PERSON - EXTERNAL ARRANGEMENT

TYPE: SPCR 48A

MK    12B

80    5621

PORT PROFILE

ENTRANCE

**NCC-6038/5**
STARBASE ONE

BOW

C

0-S

S

BG

STAR FLEET
IDENTIFICATION
PENNANT

NCC-6038/5

GRILLES

REAR PAD

STATIC GROUND LINE

S S

FWD PAD (2)

BOTTOM PLAN

BOOSTER PROPULSION (2)

GRILLES

SYM

ASE ONE

TOP PLAN

CORRUGATED COWL

OFFICIAL COLORS:

| | | |
|---|---|---|
| | PLATINUM | Nº SF 29 UC |
| BG | BLUEGRAY | Nº SF 31 UC |
| C | CORN | Nº SF 22 UC |
| S | SILVER | Nº SF 01 UC |
| | RED | Nº SF 10 UC |
| | IVORY | Nº SF 07 UC |
| | SKY BLUE | Nº SF 16 UC |
| | GRAY | Nº SF 30 UC |
| | BLACK | Nº SF 32 UC |

0    CM    1    2

METERS

ELEVATIONS:

REAR

SYM

FRONT

MAIN
PROPULSION

NCC-6038/

ASE ONE

GRILLES

GRILLES

STEP

# SHUTTLECRAFT
## INTERNAL GENERAL ARRANGEMENT

℄ CUTAWAY PROFILE

ASTROGATOR

ARRANGEMENT CLASSIFIED

STRUT

PEDESTAL

INSTRUMENTATION

FWD PAD    ENVIRONMENTAL UNIT

CEILING PLAN    SCANNER    ELECTROLUMINESCENT PANEL (3)    AFT COMPARTMENT

MAIN PROPULSION

SYM

REAR PAD

INSTRUMENTATION

OPERATOR

DECK PLAN

STEP    CHAIR (7)    SUPPORT PYLON AND STABILIZER

THROTTLES    ℄    ASTROGATOR

SCANNERS P/S

CONTROLS PANEL

LOWER DOOR

STEP

CONTROLS PEDESTAL

ELEVATION THROUGH ℄ OF ENTRANCE
LOOKING FWD

OFFICIAL COLORS:

| | | |
|---|---|---|
| | PLATINUM | N°SF 29 UC |
| | SAND | N°SF 08 UC |
| | GRAY | N°SF 30 UC |
| | OXIDE | N°SF 27 UC |
| | BLACK | N°SF 32 UC |

0    CM    1    2
METERS

# SINGLE STATEROOM
## PRIMARY HULL-CLASS I STARSHIPS

TYPICAL OFFICERS
ACCOMMODATIONS

VANITY LAVATORY

SHOWER/TUB WITH
JACUZZI UNIT

PD

BATHROOM (SHARED)

TRANSLUCENT STALL

TRANSLUCENT
STALL

WATER CLOSET

PD

LOUNGE CHAIR

WAINSCOTE
CABINET

SLEEPING
QUARTERS

PD

STD. TWIN
SIZE BED

WARDROBE

MAIN
CORRIDOR
HERE

DECORATIVE GRILLE

ROOM DIVIDER

PD

CHAIR

LIVING QUARTERS

DESK

SHIP'S SERVICES

WAINSCOTE
CABINET

PD

PD-DOUBLE POCKET DOORS

0    1    2    3
METERS

# DOUBLE STATEROOM
## PRIMARY HULL - CLASS I STARSHIPS

TYPICAL CREW
ACCOMMODATIONS

LOUNGE CHAIR

SHIP'S
SERVICES

WAINSCOTE
CABINET

LIVING
QUARTERS

DESK

CHAIR

MAIN
CORRIDOR
HERE

PD

ROOM DIVIDER

DECORATIVE GRILLE

WARDROBE

STD. TWIN
SIZE BED

WAINSCOTE
CABINET

SLEEPING
QUARTERS

PD

SHOWER/TUB WITH
JACUZZI UNIT

PD

TRANSLUCENT
STALL

BATHROOM (SHARED)

TWIN LAVATORY
VANITY

WATER CLOSET

PD

PD - DOUBLE POCKET DOORS

0      1      2      3
METERS

# MAIN BRIDGE
## DECK 1 PLAN - PRIMARY HULL - CLASS I STARSHIPS

EL - ENVIRONMENTAL SUIT LOCKER

COMMAND INTELLIGENCE
PRIMARY VISUAL DISPLAY
₵ BRIDGE
OFFSET 36°

ID - ISOLATION DOOR

KP - KICKOUT PANEL

DEFENSE SUB-SYSTEMS MONITOR

DEFENSE AND WEAPONS
STATION

OUTER SHELL
STRUCTURE

NAVIGATION
STATION

FWD

GANGWAY
(DN)

TOILET

ID

EL

ID

STEPS

EXIT

ID

COMMAND MODULE

ESSM

HANDRAIL

NAV

CHAIR

LHR

HELM

CO

ELC

SERVICE
CORRIDOR
P/S

ENVIRONMENTAL
STATION

KP

KP

COMMAND
INTELLIGENCE
STATION

ENGINEERING STATION

TURBO
ELEVATOR

PIPING AND WIRING
TRUNKS AROUND

ESSM - ENGINEERING SUB-SYSTEMS
MONITOR

COMMUNICATIONS STATION

₵
SHIP

LHR - LIMIT OF 1.90 METER HEADROOM
ELC - EDGE OF BRIDGE LIGHTING COVE

OFFICIAL COLORS:

| | | |
|---|---|---|
| | PLATINUM | N°SF29UC |
| | RED | N°SF10UC |
| | TAUPE | N°SF28UC |
| | BLACK | N°SF32UC |

0  1  2  3  4
METERS

# MAIN BRIDGE
## PRINCIPAL CROSS-SECTIONS

LONGITUDINAL-LOOKING TO PORT

TRANSVERSE-LOOKING FWD

# COMMAND MODULE
## MAIN BRIDGE STATION - CLASS I STARSHIPS

CONTROLS CONSOLE

SUPPORT PYLON

SENSORS ALERT LIGHT

TO:01:06:16

TO:01:06:17

HELMSMAN

NAVIGATOR

OPERATOR'S CHAIR

ASTROGATOR

BRIDGE VENTILATION

SHIP'S LOG AND CHRONOMETER

COM-MOD PLAT

CO CON DECK

CO CON PLAT

TO:01:06:18

COMMANDING OFFICER'S CON

50% TILE EYE-POINT

CO'S CHAIR SWIVELS FULL 360°

18° TYP.

⊕ CENTER OF BRIDGE AND ZZ' AXIS OF PRIMARY HULL

THIS STATION IS ALSO DUPLI-CATED ON THE EMERGENCY BRIDGE

OFFICIAL COLORS:

| | |
|---|---|
| PLATINUM | Nº SF 29 UC |
| ORANGE | Nº SF 11 UC |
| TAUPE | Nº SF 28 UC |
| GRAY | Nº SF 30 UC |
| BLACK | Nº SF 32 UC |

COMMUNICATIONS STATION HERE

℄ BRIDGE

0  20  40  60  80
CENTIMETERS

LOWER BRIDGE DECK

# COMMAND MODULE
## FRONT AND REAR ELEVATIONS

SHIP'S CONTROLS CONSOLE:

SENSORS ALERT LIGHT

KNEEHOLE POCKET

BRIDGE VENTILATION

OPERATOR'S CHAIR

SHIP'S CONTROLS WIRING TRUNK

REAR

₵

COM-MOD PLAT

FRONT

COMMAND CON:

COMMAND CONTROLS P/S

CO CON PLAT

CONSOLE P/S

SEE MANUAL SECTIONS 2 AND 3 FOR VITAL FUNCTIONS AND MAIN SCHEMATICS

COMMANDING OFFICER'S CON IS THE FUNCTIONAL CENTER OF THE BRIDGE. ALL OTHER STATIONS SUPPORT THIS POSITION

REAR

₵

FRONT

0  10  20  30  40  50  60  70  80
CENTIMETERS

OFFICIAL COLORS:

| | | |
|---|---|---|
| | PLATINUM | Nº SF 29 UC |
| | ORANGE | Nº SF 11 UC |
| | GRAY | Nº SF 30 UC |
| | BLACK | Nº SF 32 UC |

# HELMSMAN'S STATION
## COMMAND MODULE-MAIN BRIDGE

€ BRIDGE

SENSORS
ALERT LIGHT

SHIP'S SENSORS
ACTIVITY MONITORS

SHIP'S HELM
CONTROL PANEL

HELM SYSTEMS
STATUS BOARD

FIRE CONTROL
PANEL

COM-MOD
CONSOLE

REFER TO HELM SUBDIVISION OF THIS SECTION
FOR DETAILED OPERATIONS PROCEDURE AND
SYSTEMS FUNCTIONS SPECIFICATIONS

REFER TO ENGINEERING SECTION FOR SYSTEMS
SCHEMATICS, WIRING DIAGRAMS, AND STAND-
ARD MAINTENANCE PROCEDURES

REFER TO SECTION 01:08:00 FOR OPERATION
OF FIRE CONTROL SYSTEMS (CLASSIFIED)

FIRE CONTROL TARGET SIGHTING SYSTEM IS
HOUSED BENEATH HELM SYS. STATUS BOARD

0    5   10        20        30
|||||||||||||||||||||
CENTIMETERS

# NAVIGATOR'S STATION
## COMMAND MODULE - MAIN BRIDGE

DEVIATION PLOTTER

NAVIGATION CONTROLS

COM-MOD CONSOLE

COURSE PROGRAMMING PANEL

FIRE CONTROL PANEL

SHIP'S SENSORS ACTIVITY MONITORS

SENSORS ALERT LIGHT

₡ BRIDGE

REFER TO SECTION 02:06:00 FOR DETAILED OPERATIONS PROCEDURE AND SYSTEMS FUNCTIONS SPECIFICATIONS

REFER TO ENGINEERING SECTION FOR SYSTEMS SCHEMATICS, WIRING DIAGRAMS, AND STANDARD MAINTENANCE PROCEDURE

REFER TO SECTION 01:08:00 FOR OPERATION OF FIRE CONTROL SYSTEM (CLASSIFIED)

0    5    10        20        30
CENTIMETERS

# COMMAND CON
## COMMAND MODULE - MAIN BRIDGE

PORT CONSOLE:

COMMAND INTERCOM
PANEL

VITAL FUNCTIONS OVERRIDE PANEL

CON PIVOT CENTER

STARBOARD CONSOLE:

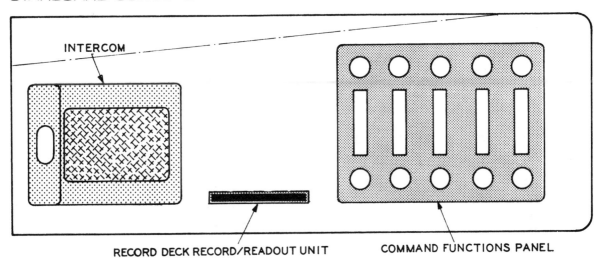

INTERCOM

RECORD DECK RECORD/READOUT UNIT

COMMAND FUNCTIONS PANEL

REFER TO SECTION 01:06:30 FOR DETAILED
OPERATIONS PROCEDURE AND SYSTEMS
FUNCTIONS SPECIFICATIONS

REFER TO ENGINEERING SECTION FOR SYS-
TEMS SCHEMATICS, WIRING DIAGRAMS, AND
STANDARD MAINTENANCE PROCEDURES

OFFICIAL COLOR:
SKY BLUE №SF16UC

0    5    10    15    20
CENTIMETERS

# ASTROGATOR
## COMMAND MODULE - MAIN BRIDGE

ASTROGATOR
HOUSING

VIEW PLATE OF
CLOUD CHAMBER

HOLOGRAPHIC
IMAGE OF M-O GALAXY

COORDINATE
GRID SYSTEM

RECORD DECK
R/R UNIT  P/S

HELM
INTERCOM PANEL

NAVIGATION
INTERCOM PANEL

INTERCOM

ASTROGATOR IS SHOWN
IN MEDIUM RESOLUTION
AND IS CENTERED ON THE
CENTER OF THE TREATY
EXPLORATION TERRITORY.
THE "FLYING POINT" BRIGHT
SPOT INDICATES THE U.F.P.
IS TARGET DESTINATION.
SHIP IS HEADING ON A BEAR-
ING OF 0 MARK 200.

SCHEMATICS, WIRING
DIAGRAMS, AND STD.
MAINTENANCE PROCE-
DURES.

THE ASTROGATOR IS
PART OF THE COURSE
TRACKING ELEMENT

VIEW SHOWN IS TRUE VIEW
OF UPPER PLANE SURFACES

SHIP'S LOG AND
CHRONOMETER

REFER TO SECTION 02:06:00
FOR DETAILED OPERATIONS PROCEDURE AND
SYSTEMS FUNCTIONS SPECIFICATIONS

REFER TO ENGINEERING SECTION FOR SYSTEMS

0  5  10     20      30      40
CENTIMETERS

# SECURITY SECTION
## PRIMARY HULL - CLASS I STARSHIPS

DECK 7 - MAIN DECK
AMIDSHIPS - PORT SIDE

CHIEF OF SECURITY

BRIEFING ROOM

CHART WALL

ISOLATION DOOR

TURBO ELEVATOR

MAIN CORRIDOR

DR

DESK

CHAIR

YEOMAN OR
WATCH OFFICER

TOILET

SECURITY OFFICE

TABLE

WARDROOM

DINETTE TABLE AND CHAIRS
(2)

TYPICAL
DETENTION CELL
(10)

MESSROOM

FOOD AND BEV. SERVICE CENTER

(CARGO HOLDS
HERE)

(MEDICAL SECTION HERE)

TOILET - TYP

ELEVATOR SHAFT

WATER CLOSET - TYP
LAVATORY - TYP

TYPICAL DOUBLE BUNKS

EXERCIZE
CORRIDOR

(MEDICAL SECTION
HERE)

0 1 2 3 4 5 6
METERS

(LIVING QUARTERS HERE)

FB - FORCE FIELD BARRIER

DR - DOOR

# HAND PHASER-TYPE I

EFF. RANGES IN METERS:
OVERLOAD BLAST RADIUS......40
DE-MATERIALIZE.........................10
DISRUPT...............................................20
HEAT..........................................................2
STUN.........................................................30

COLORS:
BR. ANTIMONY N°SF02UC
GLOSS BLACK N°SF32UC

DIM: W.O.A.....49.40 MM    D.O.A.....27.00 MM
L.O.A.....107.20 MM

ELECTRON ASPIRATOR PILE

1.02 MEV PHOTON EMITTER

TRIGGER

FRONT

FACE PLATE

DEFLECTOR SHIELD

BODY SHELL

FORCE SETTING WHEEL

FORCE INDICATOR DIAL

TOP

OPERATIONAL LIGHT (BLUE)

SIDE

ACCESS PLATE

BOTTOM

MAGNATOMIC ADHESION AREA

0   10   20   30
MILLIMETERS

BODY LINES AND SECTIONS

CENTERLINE PROFILE

PLAN

FRONT

REAR

WARNING! DISCARD ANY UNIT SHOWING ANY DIMENSIONAL CHANGE!

# HAND PHASER-TYPE II

**EFF. RANGES IN METERS:**
OVERLOAD BLAST RADIUS....135
DE-MATERIALIZE.....................30
DISRUPT.............................60
HEAT....................................6
STUN.................................90

**DIM:**
L.O.A.....221.00 MM
W.O.A.....49.40 MM
D.O.A.....157.50 MM

BEAM SHIELD (P)

BEAM EMITTER

PHOTON ACCELERATOR

DILITHIUM CRYSTAL CELL

FORWARD LOCKPLATE

DEFLECTOR SHIELD

HAND PHASER TYPE I LOCKED-ON (REQUIRED)

FIRING TRIGGERS

GRIP

MAGNATOMIC ADHESION AREAS

REAR LOCKPLATE

LOCK RELEASE

SECT. A-A

FORCE SETTING DIAL

DEFLECTOR SHIELD

0  10  20  30
MILLIMETERS

**COLORS:**
BR. ANTIMONY №SF02UC
GL. BLUEGRAY №SF31UC
GLOSS BLACK №SF32UC
(P) CLEAR WHITE TOPAZ

# HAND PHASER-TYPE II

LOCKPLATE RECESS

RECESS TO MATCH
FACEPLATE OF HAND
PHASER TYPE I

FWD LOCKPLATE DTL.

FREE
POSITION

REAR LOCKPLATE
DETAIL

0    10    20    30
MILLIMETERS

LINES AND
SECTIONS

X

STRAIGHT
LINE
TRANSITION
HERE

B

B

INTERLOCKING
SWITCH

S

S T

S=SAFETY    T=TRIGGER
TRIGGER DETAIL

GRIP
ATTACHMENT
TO BODY

VIEW B-B

WARNING! DISCARD ANY UNIT SHOWING ANY DIMENSIONAL CHANGE!

# RAY GUN
## OFFENSIVE/DEFENSIVE AREA WEAPON

SPECIFICATION:
MODEL: TYPE I
OFFENSIVE (DISRUPT) RANGE (M)_____90
EFFECTIVE AREA AT RANGE (M)_____3
DEFENSIVE (STUN) RANGE (M)_____180
EFFECTIVE AREA AT RANGE (M)_____8
LENGTH OVERALL (CM)_____23.5
MAXIMUM DIAMETER (CM)_____8.4
WEIGHT (GM)_____630

DIAMOND EMITTER TUBE

COLLETTE

SIDE VIEW

BODY HOUSING

FRONT VIEW

TRIGGERS:
OFFENSIVE
DEFENSIVE

COLORS:
TRANSLUCENT
ANTIMONY NºSF02UC
GRAY      NºSF30UC
BLACK     NºSF32UC

0  1  2  3  4  5
CENTIMETERS

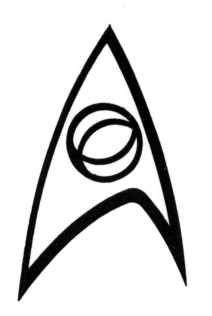

# SCIENCES SECTION

NOTE (*). NO CURRENT PRINT-OUT FROM MASTERCOM DATABANKS/SFHQ

## SECTION INDEX

| TO. NO: | SUBJECT | CURRENT | REPLACES |
|---|---|---|---|
| 02:00:05 | SECTION INDEX | 7309.10 | |
| » :11:12 | ANABOLIC PROTOPLASER - LARGE VERSION | 7503.04 | |
| » » :13 | » » - SMALL VERSION | » | |
| » » :14 | SURGICAL SCALPELS | 7503.03 | |

NOTE (*): NO CURRENT PRINT-OUT FROM MASTERCOM DATABANKS/SFHQ

# COMMAND INTELLIGENCE
## MAIN BRIDGE STATION - CLASS I STARSHIPS

FRONT ELEVATION

VIEW A-A:

110° SCAN

CIRCULAR ARC BACK

50%TILE EYEPOINT

90° SCAN

CONTROLS CONSOLE

BRIDGE VENTILATION

OPERATOR'S CHAIR

RAILING

MAIN BRIDGE DECK

NOTE:  CD-COMPUTER DATA AND SYSTEMS
VISUAL READ-OUT SCREENS

THIS STATION IS ALSO DUPLICATED ON
THE EMERGENCY BRIDGE

ALL SCIENTIFIC COMMAND INTELLIGENCE
IS HANDLED THROUGH THIS STATION

SEE TO:02:01:01 FOR CONTROLS CONSOLE
ARRANGEMENT

OFFICIAL COLORS:

| | | |
|---|---|---|
| | PLATINUM | N°SF29UC |
| | RED | N°SF10UC |
| | GRAY | N°SF30UC |
| | BLACK | N°SF32UC |

VISUAL INTELLIGENCE DISPLAY

VISUAL INTELLIGENCE DISPLAY

CD

CD

CD

CD

CD

CD

CD

CD

0  20  40  60  80
CENTIMETERS

# CONTROLS CONSOLE
VIEW B-B OF TO:02:01:00

REFER ELSEWHERE IN THIS SECTION FOR
DETAILED OPERATIONS PROCEDURES,
AND SYSTEMS FUNCTIONS SPECIFICA-
TIONS.

REFER TO ENGINEERING SECTION FOR
SYSTEMS SCHEMATICS, WIRING DIA-
GRAMS, AND STANDARD MAINTENANCE
PROCEDURES.

COMMAND INTELLIGENCE
SYSTEMS RECORD DECKS
STORAGE

SCIENCES AND TECHNOLOGY
FUNCTIONS PATCH-IN PANEL

COMMAND INTELLIGENCE
VISUAL DISPLAY COMPLEX
CONTROL PANEL

SCIENCES DIVISION INTERCOM

COMMAND INTERCOM

CENTROID OF STATION

COMPUTER AUDIO OUTPUT

CENTROID OF
SEATED BODY

BRIDGE INTERCOM

ACTIVE RECORD DECKS HOLDER

LIBRARY COMPUTER
CONTROL PANEL

SHIP'S SENSORS AND SCANNERS
COMPLEX CONTROL PANEL

INTERCOM STATION

COMMAND FUNCTIONS SLAVE
PANEL

TYPE SS-HRS/RVS-I SCANNER

OFFICIAL COLORS:
BLUE   N°SF 16 UC
BLACK N°SF 32 UC

0  10  20  30  40  50
CENTIMETERS

# SCIENCES TRICORDER

## TYPE I

SELECTIVELY SENSE, MEASURE, ANALYZE, COMPARE, AND
IDENTIFY SURROUNDING ENVIRONMENTAL CONDITION.
MULTIPLE CHANNEL RECORD OR READOUT CAPABILITY
WITH MULTI-MODE DISPLAY CHOICE.

OFFICIAL COLORS:

| | | |
|---|---|---|
| | ANTIMONY | № SF 02 UC |
| | OLIVE | № SF 14 UC |
| | BLACK | № SF 32 UC |

℄ SYMMETRY

DISPLAY-CONTROL
HEAD COVER

RECORD-COMPARE
SECTION LID

CIRCUITRY-POWER SUPPLY
SECTION (IN BODY)

(PEBBLED)

DISPLAY HEAD OPEN

127 CM LONG
NAUGAHYDE
SHOULDER
STRAP

SIDE BODY
STORAGE
SHELLS

CASE
FRAMES
(BRUSHED)

(PEBBLED)

FULL SIZE. DIMENSIONS: H.O.A.(CLOSED) ~ 177.8 MM;  W.O.A. ~ 114.3 MM;  D.O.A. ~ 48.3 MM;

# SCIENCES TRICORDER
## ARRANGEMENT - UNIT OPEN

### TYPE I

OPEN D/C SECTION ACTIVATES UNIT

VIDEO DISPLAY

WIRE HARNESS DUCT EACH SIDE

NC10-32/4 OVAL HD. SCREW EACH SIDE

FRAME MEMBER

REMOVABLE PLAY/RECORD DISCS (8)

COMPRESSION PLATE

DISC HOLDER FRAME

DISC SELECTOR W/LIGHT

MATCHED COMPARISON LIGHT (BLUE)

SENSOR ARRAY

SUB-NORMAL LIGHT (AMBER)

FACEPLATE

DANGER-ALARM LIGHT (RED)

RECORD/PLAY W/VOL. & LIGHT

SEE NOTE D

CHANNEL SEL. W/LIGHT

SPEAKER/MIC.

FACEPLATE

NOTE D: THIS ROW OF LIGHTS (GREEN)

LID OPEN

THIS SECTION TO BE OPENED ONLY BY CLASS A SPECIALIST RATINGS

TYPICAL SECTION

1.27 MM

FULL SIZE

LOWER CATCH DETAIL

# SCIENCES TRICORDER
## INTERNAL ARRANGEMENT*

TYPE I

SENSOR ARRAY:
DENSITY – GAS – PRESSURE – RADIATION –
SPECTRAL – AND THERMAL SENSORS.

VIEW A-A

VIEW B-B

*20TH CENTURY SUBSTITUTE. ACTUAL IS CLASSIFIED BY SFAF PRIME DIRECTIVE.

# SCIENCES TRICORDER

## CASE DETAILS

TYPE I

CONTROL HEAD SECTION

VIEW D-D

SENSOR ARRAY

℄ PIVOT

VIEW C-C

SPRING CATCH EA. SIDE

3.08 MM

18.54 MM

LOCK SLOTS

VIDEO DISPLAY CUTOUT

5 MM GRID

VIDEO/CONTROLS FACEPLATE

VIEW E-E

4.80 MM DIA (6)

THREAD NC 10-32-3A

BORE 12.72 MM DIA

UNIT ACTIVATING SPST SWITCH

HUB: 12.70 MM O.D.
10.16 MM I.D.

CASE

LOCK OPEN DIMPLE

PICKUP CTR. FROM CASE

℄ SYM. CASE

LOCK CLOSED DIMPLE

NF 2-56/2 FLAT HD. SCREW (4)

WIRE HARNESS PASS THROUGH HOLE EA. SIDE

NF 4-40/4 FLAT HD. BODY ATTACH SCREW (11)

VIEW F-F

CRYSTAL SHELL

CHAMFER 45° x 1 MM

5.58MM

31.75 MM

INERT CORE

RECORD/PLAY DISC

2.54 MM THK FRAME

3 MM DIA. VENT HOLES 11 EA. SIDE

LOWER CATCH STUD

ALSO REFER TO
TO:02:11:03

FULL SIZE

# GALACTIC COORD. SYSTEM
### GREAT SPIRAL MILKY WAY GALAXY M-O

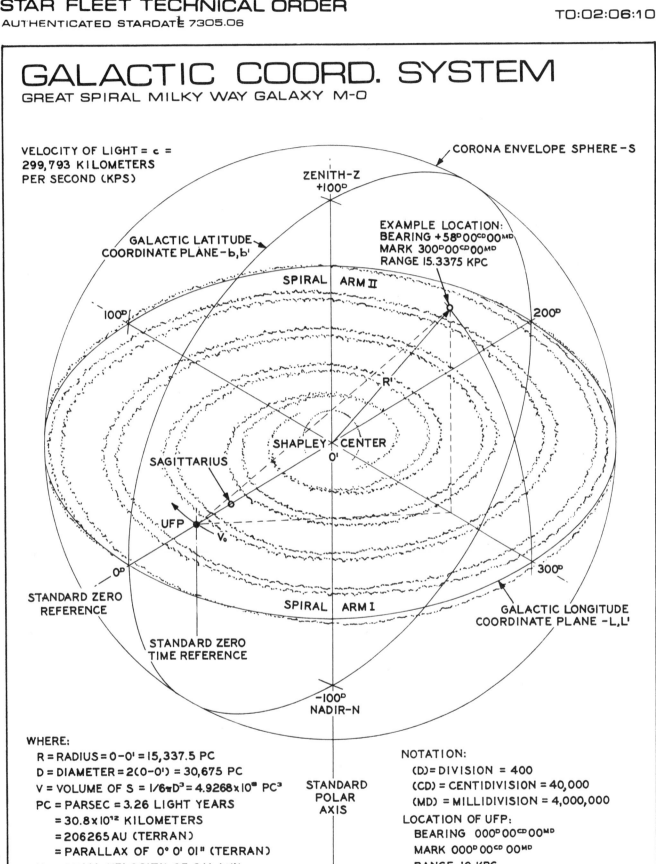

VELOCITY OF LIGHT = c =
299,793 KILOMETERS
PER SECOND (KPS)

CORONA ENVELOPE SPHERE—S

GALACTIC LATITUDE
COORDINATE PLANE—b,b'

ZENITH—Z
+100ᴰ

EXAMPLE LOCATION:
BEARING +58ᴰ00ᶜᴰ00ᴹᴰ
MARK 300ᴰ00ᶜᴰ00ᴹᴰ
RANGE 15.3375 KPC

SPIRAL ARM II

100ᴰ

200ᴰ

R'

SHAPLEY CENTER
O'

SAGITTARIUS

UFP

V₀

0ᴰ

300ᴰ

STANDARD ZERO
REFERENCE

SPIRAL ARM I

GALACTIC LONGITUDE
COORDINATE PLANE—L,L'

STANDARD ZERO
TIME REFERENCE

−100ᴰ
NADIR—N

STANDARD
POLAR
AXIS

POLARIS II
GALAXY

WHERE:
R = RADIUS = 0-0' = 15,337.5 PC
D = DIAMETER = 2(0-0') = 30,675 PC
V = VOLUME OF S = 1/6πD³ = 4.9268×10⁸ PC³
PC = PARSEC = 3.26 LIGHT YEARS
    = 30.8×10¹² KILOMETERS
    = 206265 AU (TERRAN)
    = PARALLAX OF 0° 0' 01" (TERRAN)
V₀ = AXIAL VELOCITY OF GALAXY
    = 267.5 KPS AT RADIUS OF UFP
UFP = UNITED FEDERATION OF PLANETS
AU = ASTRONOMICAL UNIT (TERRAN)
R' = RANGE IN PC OR KPC (PC×1000)

NOTATION:
    (D) = DIVISION = 400
    (CD) = CENTIDIVISION = 40,000
    (MD) = MILLIDIVISION = 4,000,000
LOCATION OF UFP:
    BEARING 000ᴰ00ᶜᴰ00ᴹᴰ
    MARK 000ᴰ00ᶜᴰ00ᴹᴰ
    RANGE 10 KPC
    STATED AS:" 0 MARK 0 −R 10 KPC"

# S.I.N.S.* BASE DATUM
## IN GALACTIC COORDINATE SYSTEM

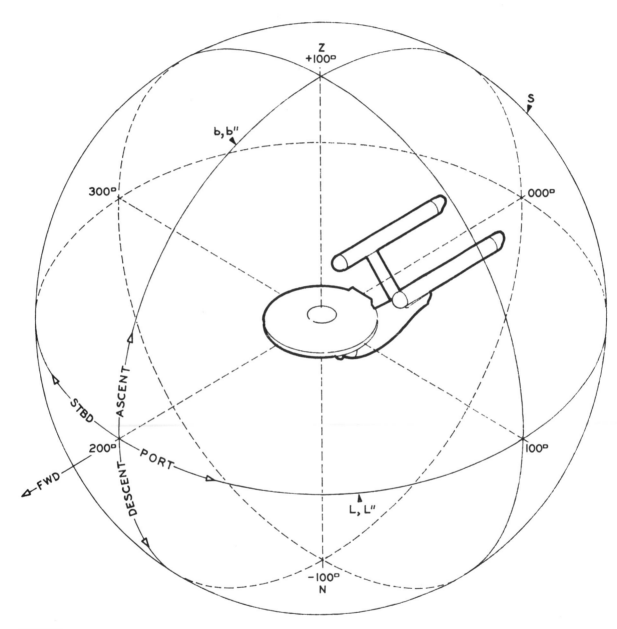

WHERE:

    THE SPACE·INERTIAL·NAVIGATION·SYSTEM* IS THE FUNDAMENTAL GUIDANCE BASE FOR THE ONBOARD NAVIGATIONAL COMPUTER COMPLEX. IT IS ACTIVATED AND ACCURATELY ALIGNED IN THE GALACTIC COORDINATE SYSTEM AT COMMISSIONING IN PLANETARY ORBIT AND THERE-AFTER MAINTAINS THIS ALIGNMENT WITHOUT ERROR. THE STARSHIP CARRIES THIS DATUM WITH IT (FWD) WHEREVER IT GOES AND MOVES WITHIN THIS REFERENCE FRAMEWORK: TO PORT OR STARBOARD AND UP OR DOWN IN ANY COMBINATION.

b, b″ – DECLINATION PLANE
L, L″ – AZIMUTH PLANE
N – NADIR AT b, b″ –100°
Z – ZENITH AT b, b″ +100°

S – SPHERICAL ENVELOPE CONTAINING ALL
    NUMERICAL COMBINATIONS OF b, b″ & L, L″

# COURSE TRACKING ELEMENT
## SCHEMATIC DIAGRAM - CLASS I STARSHIPS

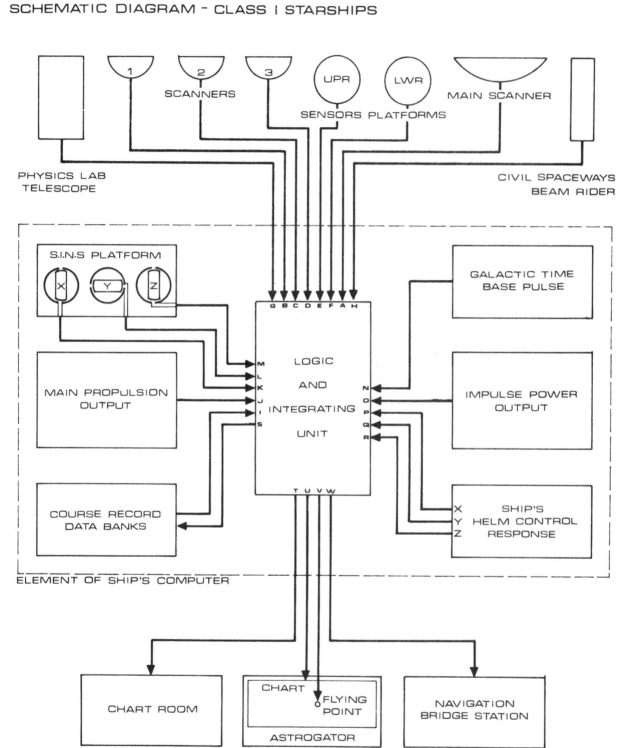

THE COURSE TRACKING ELEMENT IS THE VITAL HEART OF THE STARSHIP'S NAVIGATION
SYSTEM. IT IS ACTIVATED UPON COMMISIONING IN PLANETARY ORBIT AND THEREAFTER IT
MAINTAINS AN ACCURATE CONSTANT RECORD AND PLOT OF THE SHIP'S COURSE AND LOCA-
TION WITHIN THE GALAXY. FROM ANY LOCATION IT WILL GIVE A DIRECT BEARING TO THE
SHIP'S HOME BASE, ITS DESTINATION, OR ANY OTHER DIVERSIONARY POINT.

# VELOCITY/TIME RELATIONSHIP
## INTERSTELLAR SPACE/WARP TECHNOLOGY

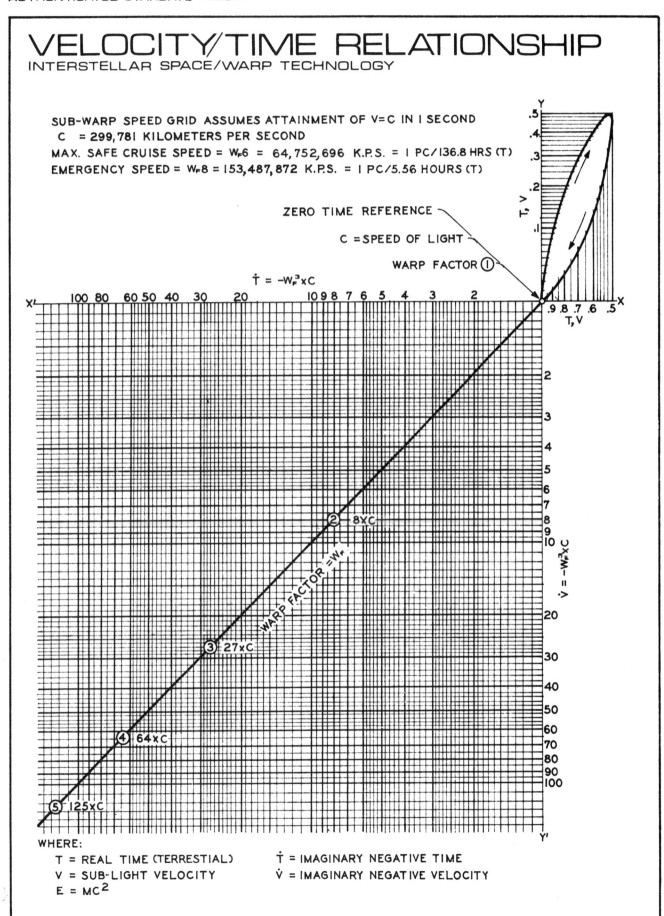

SUB-WARP SPEED GRID ASSUMES ATTAINMENT OF V=C IN I SECOND
C = 299,781 KILOMETERS PER SECOND
MAX. SAFE CRUISE SPEED = $W_F6$ = 64,752,696 K.P.S. = I PC/136.8 HRS (T)
EMERGENCY SPEED = $W_F8$ = 153,487,872 K.P.S. = I PC/5.56 HOURS (T)

ZERO TIME REFERENCE
C = SPEED OF LIGHT
WARP FACTOR ①

$\dot{T} = -W_F^3 \times C$

$\dot{V} = -W_F^3 \times C$

WARP FACTOR = $W_F$

② 8XC
③ 27XC
④ 64XC
⑤ 125XC

WHERE:
T = REAL TIME (TERRESTIAL)          $\dot{T}$ = IMAGINARY NEGATIVE TIME
V = SUB-LIGHT VELOCITY              $\dot{V}$ = IMAGINARY NEGATIVE VELOCITY
$E = MC^2$

# STANDARD ORBITS
## CLASS I STARSHIPS

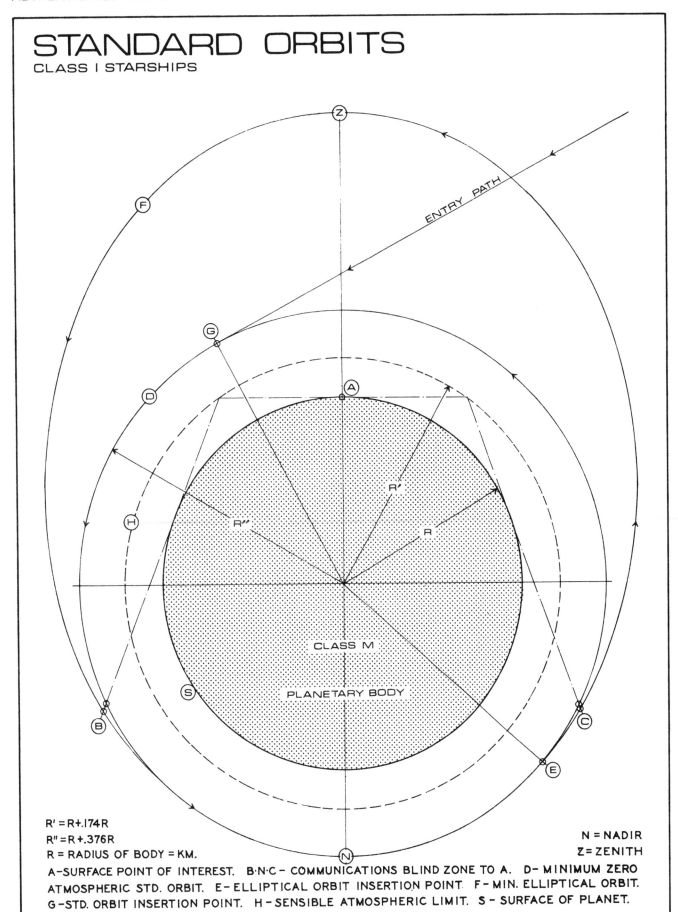

R' = R+.174R
R" = R+.376R
R = RADIUS OF BODY = KM.

N = NADIR
Z = ZENITH

A - SURFACE POINT OF INTEREST.   B·N·C - COMMUNICATIONS BLIND ZONE TO A.   D - MINIMUM ZERO
ATMOSPHERIC STD. ORBIT.   E - ELLIPTICAL ORBIT INSERTION POINT.   F - MIN. ELLIPTICAL ORBIT.
G - STD. ORBIT INSERTION POINT.   H - SENSIBLE ATMOSPHERIC LIMIT.   S - SURFACE OF PLANET.

# MILKY WAY GALAXY
## GREAT SPIRAL GALAXY - M-0 - LOCAL GROUP

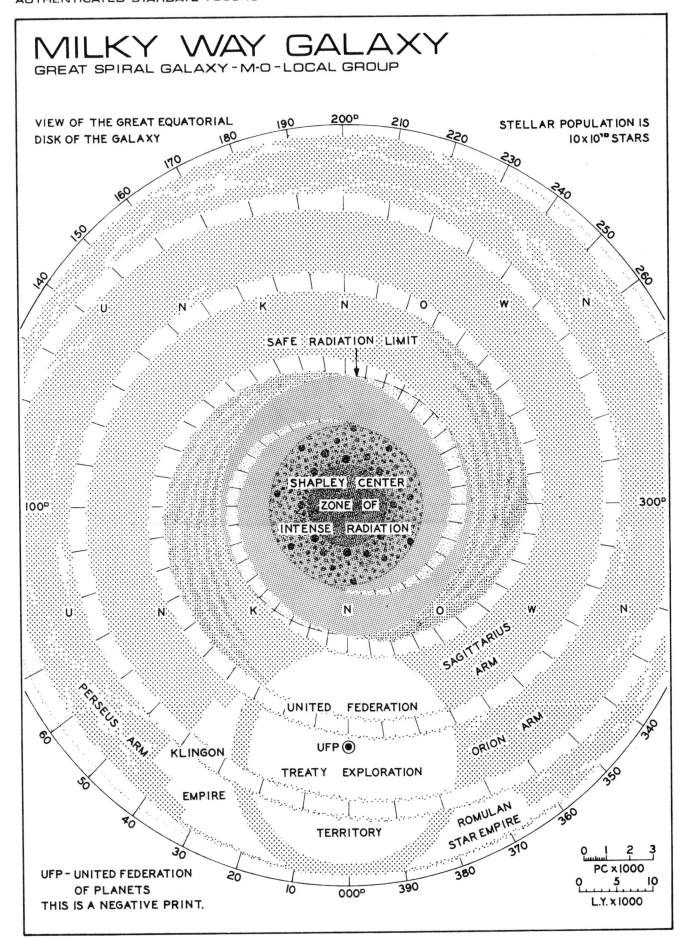

VIEW OF THE GREAT EQUATORIAL
DISK OF THE GALAXY

STELLAR POPULATION IS
10 x 10$^{10}$ STARS

190  200$^D$  210
180  220
170  230
160  240
150  250
140  260

U   N   K   N   O   W   N

SAFE RADIATION LIMIT

SHAPLEY CENTER
ZONE OF
INTENSE RADIATION

100$^D$   300$^D$

U   N   K   N   O   W   N

SAGITTARIUS ARM

PERSEUS ARM

UNITED FEDERATION

UFP ⊙

TREATY EXPLORATION

ORION ARM

KLINGON

EMPIRE

TERRITORY

ROMULAN
STAR EMPIRE

60
50
40
30
20
10
000$^D$   390   380   370   360   350   340

0 1 2 3
PC x 1000

0   5   10
L.Y. x 1000

UFP - UNITED FEDERATION
OF PLANETS
THIS IS A NEGATIVE PRINT.

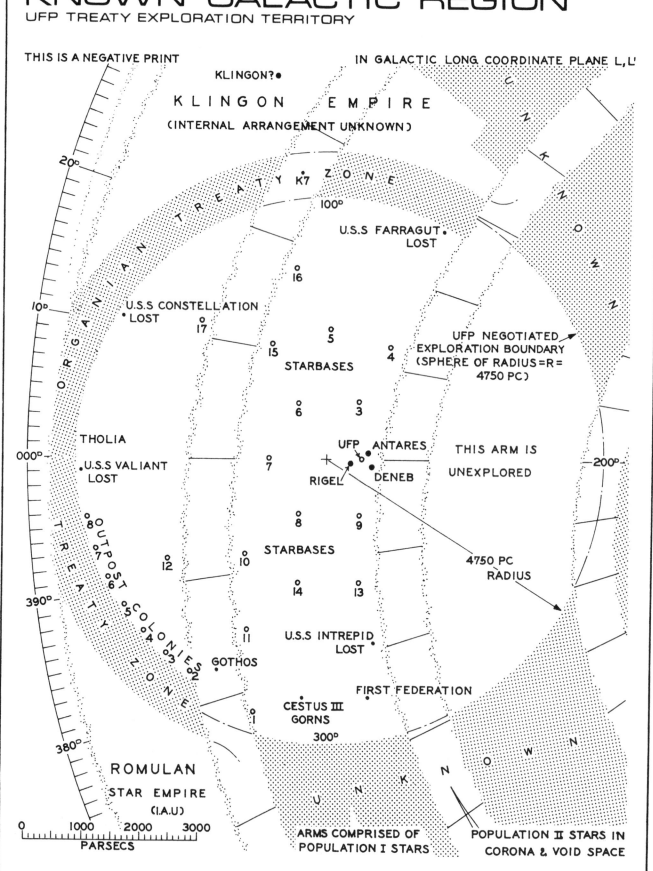

# UNITED FEDERATION
## OF PLANETS - PRINCIPAL STELLAR SYSTEMS

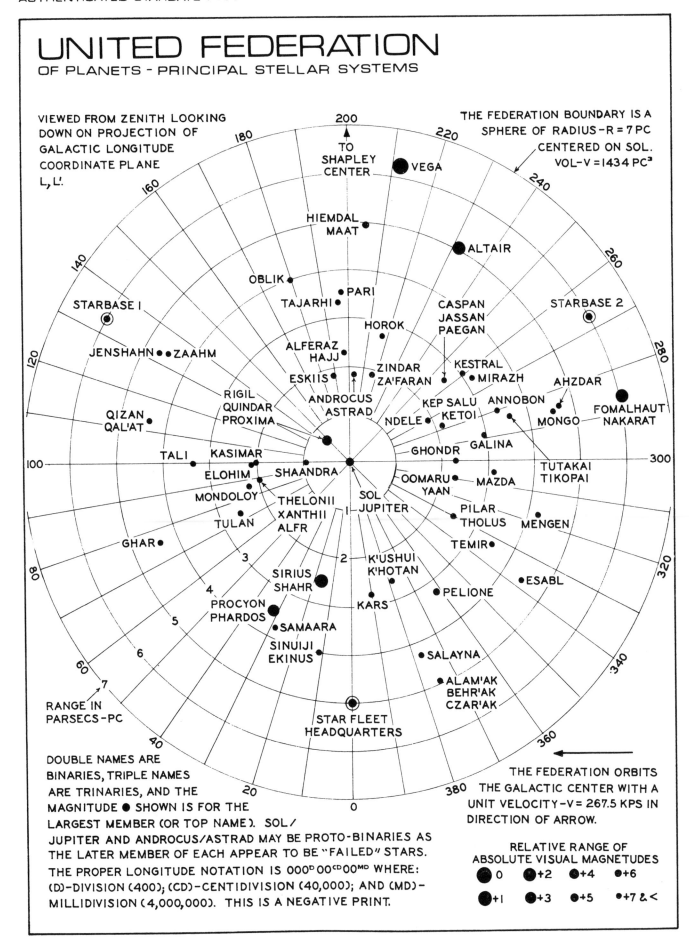

VIEWED FROM ZENITH LOOKING DOWN ON PROJECTION OF GALACTIC LONGITUDE COORDINATE PLANE L, L'.

THE FEDERATION BOUNDARY IS A SPHERE OF RADIUS-R = 7 PC CENTERED ON SOL. VOL-V = 1434 PC³

RANGE IN PARSECS-PC

DOUBLE NAMES ARE BINARIES, TRIPLE NAMES ARE TRINARIES, AND THE MAGNITUDE ● SHOWN IS FOR THE LARGEST MEMBER (OR TOP NAME). SOL/ JUPITER AND ANDROCUS/ASTRAD MAY BE PROTO-BINARIES AS THE LATER MEMBER OF EACH APPEAR TO BE "FAILED" STARS. THE PROPER LONGITUDE NOTATION IS 000ᴰ00ᶜᴰ00ᴹᴰ WHERE: (D)-DIVISION (400); (CD)-CENTIDIVISION (40,000); AND (MD)- MILLIDIVISION (4,000,000). THIS IS A NEGATIVE PRINT.

THE FEDERATION ORBITS THE GALACTIC CENTER WITH A UNIT VELOCITY-V = 267.5 KPS IN DIRECTION OF ARROW.

RELATIVE RANGE OF ABSOLUTE VISUAL MAGNETUDES
● 0  ● +2  ● +4  ● +6
● +1  ● +3  ● +5  ● +7 & <

# MEDICAL SECTION
## DECK 7 - PLAN - PRIMARY HULL - CLASS I STARSHIPS

CONVALESCENT WARD
DUTY NURSES QUARTERS
WAITING ROOM

TYPICAL BATHROOM
THERAPEUTIC BATHS
DENTAL UNIT

FWD

SHIP'S COMPUTER AND
EMERGENCY BRIDGE

PORT

STBD

SHIP'S SERVICE
MEDICAL RESEARCH LAB
DOCTORS OFFICES
BIO-CHEMICAL LAB

OBSTETRICS
TURBO-ELEVATOR SHAFT

LONG C

| | |
|---|---|
| Ⓐ ASEPTIC ENTRY LOBBY | Ⓚ DUTY DOCTOR'S OFFICE |
| Ⓑ SECTION ISOLATION DOOR (6) | Ⓛ DUTY DOCTOR'S LABORATORY |
| Ⓒ MEDICAL SECTION CORRIDOR | Ⓖ GANGWAY - P/S -UP/DOWN |
| Ⓓ EXAMINATION/OPERATING ROOM | Ⓝ DUTY NURSE/RECEPTION CENTER |
| Ⓔ TURBO-ELEVATOR CAR | Ⓞ MEDICAL SUPPLY ROOM |
| Ⓕ INTENSIVE CARE UNIT | |
| Ⓗ CHIEF SURGEON'S OFFICE | |
| Ⓙ CHIEF SURGEON'S LABORATORY | |

0 2 4 6 8 10 12 14 16 18 20
METERS

# MEDICAL TRICORDER
## STANDARD FIELD EQUIPMENT ITEM - TYPE I

SPECIFICATION:
L.O.A.-177.8MM___W.O.A-114.3MM___D.O.A.-48.3MM___WT.-900GM

DISPLAY HEAD OPEN

DISPLAY - CONTROL HEAD COVER

RECORD - COMPARE SECTION LID

ANALYZER COMPARTMENT LID

127CM LONG NAUGAHYDE SHOULDER STRAP

SIDE STORAGE BODY SHELLS

CASE FRAMES (BRUSHED)

₵ SYM

COLORS:
☐ ANTIMONY N₀SF02UC
▨ OLIVE N₀SF14UC
▦ BLACK N₀SF32UC (PEBBLED)

0  1  2  3  4  5
CENTIMETERS

# MEDICAL TRICORDER
## OPEN ARRANGEMENT

OPEN D/C SECTION ACTIVATES UNIT

VIDEO DISPLAY

Ⓐ MATCHED COMPARISON (BLUE) L.E.D.

Ⓑ SUB-NORMAL (AMBER) L.E.D.

Ⓒ DANGER-ALARM (RED) L.E.D.

ATTACH SCREW (2) SEE T.O:02:04:01

Ⓓ DISC SELECTOR CONTROL W/(GREEN) L.E.D.

FRAME MEMBER

REMOVABLE PLAY/ RECORD DISCS (8) SEE T.O:02:04:03

Ⓔ CHANNEL SELECTOR CONTROL W/(GREEN) L.E.D.

COMPRESSION PLATE

DISC HOLDER PLATE

R/P SECT. LID (OPEN)

Ⓕ RECORD/PLAY CONT. W/VOL. & (GREEN) L.E.D.

LIFE FORM FUNCTIONS SENSOR/ANALYZER

Ⓖ WIRE HARNESS DUCT EACH SIDE

Ⓗ SPEAKER-MICROPHONE

Ⓙ FACEPLATE

LOWER COMPARTMENT LID (PARTIALLY OPEN)

SEE T.O:02:04:01 FOR FRAME SECTION & LOWER CATCH DETAIL

SENSOR ARRAY

0 1 2 3 4 5
CENTIMETERS

# MEDICAL TRICORDER
## INTERNAL ARRANGEMENT

SELECTIVELY MEASURE, COMPARE, AND DIAGNOSE LIFE FORM
VITAL SIGNS, ALSO SENSE, MEASURE, AND COMPARE HEALTH
CONDITION OF ENVIRONMENT.  24 CHANNEL CAPABILITY IN-
PUT OR RECORD WITH MULTI-MODE DISPLAY READOUT.

SENSOR ARRAY

VIDEO DISPLAY

L.E.D. PILOTS

CONTROLS
W/L.E.D'S

VIDEO
HARNESS

FRAME MEMBER

SPRING
PANEL

PANEL LIGHT

CONTROLS
HARNESS

SPKR/MIC
TYPE 32-0214

RECORD/PLAY
DISC (8)

CH. 3
PICKUP (8)

CH. I PICKUP (8)

CH. 2
PICKUP (8)

UPPER LID

INTERNAL
CIRCUITRY IS
CLASSIFIED

SENSOR/
ANALYZER FOR
LIFE FORMS

ENERGY PAK

LOWER LID

0   1   2   3   4   5
CENTIMETERS

# MEDICAL TRICORDER
DETAILS

ALSO REFER TO
TO:02:04:03

CONTROLS HARNESS    VIDEO UNIT    DISC SEL.    ON-OFF SW W/VOL

STRAP SLOT
SIDE SHELL

SIDE FRAME    CLIP (4)    SENSOR ARRAY / VIDEO HARNESS
SIGNAL L.E.D'S

CHANNEL 2 PICKUPS    HARNESS    BODY SHELL

SPEAKER/MIC

CHANNEL 1 PICKUPS

HEAD

ANALYZER COMPARTMENT    DISC HOLDER    LID    GRILLE
LID HINGE

BODY

RECORD/PLAY SCHEMATIC:

DISC: (1)    (2)    (3)    (4)    (5)    (6)    (7)    (8) DISC SELECTOR

(3)
(2)
(1)
CHANNEL PICKUPS    CHANNEL SELECTOR    INPUT
OR
OUTPUT

130 CM FREE LENGTH

SENSOR/ANALYZER

0    1    2    3    4    5
CENTIMETERS

# HEARTBEAT READER
## STAR FLEET COLLEGE OF MEDICINE STANDARD

USED TO INSTANTANEOUSLY READ
THE INDIVIDUAL OR COLLECTIVE
HEARTBEATS OF ONE OR A GROUP
OF INTELLIGENT LIFE FORMS

GROUP READINGS ARE USEFUL
IN DETERMING NORMS FOR
NEWLY DISCOVERED LIFE FORMS
OR FOR DETECTING AN ALIEN LIFE
FORM DISGUISED IN A KNOWN GROUP

MODEL: SFAF/SG-MK06-TYPE M

GUARD AND ANTI-STRAY
AUDIBLE NOISE SCREEN

CLAMP BAND

GROUND PLANE SCREEN

OMNIDIRECTIONAL SENSOR

MULTIPLE READING
CANCEL INDICATOR

DIGITAL READOUT WITH
FLOATING DECIMAL

UNIT GO INDICATOR

SLIDE SWITCHES

OFF
ACTIVATE

OFF
AUDIBLE

BPM

SPECIFICATION:
LENGTH OVERALL (CM)_ _ _ _17.75
MAXIMUM DIAMETER (CM) _ _ _5.2
WEIGHT (GM) _ _ _ _ _ _ _ _230

TO IDENTIFY AN ALIEN IN A GROUP  HOLD
UNIT CLOSE TO FIRST INDIVIDUAL AND
REDUCE MULTIPLE SELECTOR UNTIL
CANCEL INDICATOR GOES OUT. THAT
HEARTBEAT IS NOW REMOVED FROM GROUP
READING. CANCEL INDICATOR WILL GLOW
AGAIN WHEN UNIT IS MOVED TO ANOTHER
INDIVIDUAL. REPEAT PROCESS UNTIL
FLUCTUATING READOUT AND AUDIBLE IS
REMOVED, OR IS LAST REMAINING
INDIVIDUAL IN GROUP

BODY SHELL

SECTION

END VIEW

SOLO/MULTIPLE
READING SELECTOR

S    M
SAMPLE

VOL
0    10

AUDIBLE VOLUME CONTROL

COLORS:
 BLUE ⎫
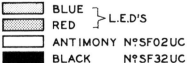 RED  ⎬ L.E.D'S
☐ ANTIMONY №SF02UC
■ BLACK    №SF32UC

0    1    2    3    4
CENTIMETERS

# SPRAY APPLICATOR
## STAR FLEET COLLEGE OF MEDICINE STANDARD

THIS DISPENSER IS USED TO APPLY
EXTERNAL MEDICATIONS, ANTIBIOTICS,
AND PROTECTIVE DRESSINGS TO SMALL
WOUNDS AND CONTUSIONS

SPECIFICATION:
      MODEL: SFAF/SG-MK01-70
      SIZE: 70
      LENGTH OVERALL-LOADED (CM)_ _6.5
      MAXIMUM DIAMETER (CM)_ _ _ _ _ _1.9
      WEIGHT-LOADED (GM)_ _ _ _ _ _ _160

(A) APPLICATOR BODY

(B) SPRAY TRIGGER (PRESS TO SPRAY)

(C) INTERCHANGABLE VIAL

(D) DISPENSING TEAT

(E) INTERCHANGABLE NOZZLE

NOZZLES AVAILABLE:
      SIZE:               ORIFICE DIA/MM
      EXTRA FINE_ _ _ _ _ _ _ _ _ _ _.0025
      FINE_ _ _ _ _ _ _ _ _ _ _ _ _ _ _.025
      MEDIUM _ _ _ _ _ _ _ _ _ _ _ _ _.20
      COARSE_ _ _ _ _ _ _(SPECIAL ORDER)

TRANSPARENT PRESSURIZED VIAL. REFER
TO UNIFORM PHARMACEUTICALS CODE
SPECIFICATION FOR PRELOADED VIALS
AVAILABLE FROM STANDARD STOCK

SPECIFICATION:
      FLUID CAPACITY (CC)_ _ _ _ _ _ _70
      WEIGHT-LOADED (GM) _ _ _ _ _ _80
      PRESSURIZED TO (KG/CM$^2$)_ _._ _1.30

COLORS:
      ANTIMONY N$\underline{o}$SF02UC BASIC. OTHERWISE
      MATCHES COLOR CODE OF VIAL CONTENTS

0   1   2   3   4
CENTIMETERS

# MEDICAL SCANNER
## STAR FLEET COLLEGE OF MEDICINE STANDARD

USED FOR FIELD DETERMINATION OF GEN.
MEDICAL CONDITION OF INTELLIGENT
LIFE FORMS BY SENSING BODY EMANATIONS
IN EMISSION GROUPS OF: ALPHA, BETA,
GAMMA, KIRLIAN, THETA, AND XI RAYS

REFER TO COLLEGE OF MEDICINE STD.
DIAGNOSTIC PRACTISES JOURNAL FOR
SCALE CALIBRATIONS AND CURRENT
INTERPRETATIONG OF READINGS

SPECIFICATION:
    LENGTH OVERALL (CM)_ _ _ _ _ _ 6.05
    MAXIMUM DIAMETER (CM)_ _ _ _ _ _ 3.5
    WEIGHT (GM)_ _ _ _ _ _ _ _ _ _ _ 230
    SENSITIVITY (EmV/AU²)_ _ _ _ _TO .0001
    READING GROUPS_ _ _ _ _A, B, Γ, K, Θ, Ξ

ROT 180° CW

Ⓐ COMPUTER HOUSING

Ⓑ ACTIVATING SWITCH (PRESS ON-OFF)

Ⓒ SCANNER HOUSING (48 MESH SCREEN)

Ⓓ ROTATING SCANNER

Ⓔ READINGS DIAL (INCREASE FROM
   BOTTOM TO TOP)

Ⓕ LIFE FORM TYPE SELECTION SCALE

Ⓖ GROUND PLANE SCREEN (48 MESH)

Ⓗ NT - NORMAL TERRAN RANGE

COLORS:
    ☐ ANTIMONY Nº SF02UC
    ▨ GRAY     Nº SF30UC
    ■ BLACK    Nº SF32UC

0  1  2  3  4
CENTIMETERS

# ANABOLIC PROTOPLASER
## STAR FLEET COLLEGE OF MEDICINE STANDARD

PORTABLE WOUND HEALER. MINOR
INJURY VERSION. STANDARD FIELD
EQUIPMENT UNIT.

SPECIFICATION:
    MODEL: SFAF/SG-MK08-0
    SIZE: 0
    INTENSITY SCALE: 0-100 EmV/AU$^2$
    LENGTH OVERALL (CM) _ _ _ _ _ _25
    WIDTH OVERALL (CM)_ _ _ _ _ _ _3.8
    HEIGHT OVERALL (CM)_ _ _ _ _ _4.2
    WEIGHT (GM)_ _ _ _ _ _ _ _ _ _450

(A) HOUSING

(B) REMOVABLE BOTTOM PANEL

(C) SPECIFICATIONS PLATE

(D) ACTIVATING SWITCH AND INTENSITY
    CONTROL - DEPRESS TO OPERATE

(E) EFFECTIVITY SENSOR

(F) DNA MATCH SYNTHESIZATION UNIT

(G) RAY EMISSION DUCT

(H) RECHARGING CHAMBER

(J) INTENSITY FORCE LIGHT:

| 0 | 25 | 50 | 75 | 100 |
|---|----|----|----|-----|
| OFF | | SCALE | | FULL |

TOP
PLAN

ROT 90° CCW

FRONT
ELEVATION

SIDE
PROFILE

COLORS:

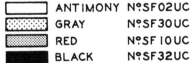

| | ANTIMONY | N°SF02UC |
|---|----------|----------|
| | GRAY | N°SF30UC |
| | RED | N°SF10UC |
| | BLACK | N°SF32UC |

0  1  2  3  4  5  6
CENTIMETERS

# ANABOLIC PROTOPLASER
## STAR FLEET COLLEGE OF MEDICINE STANDARD

PORTABLE WOUND HEALER – MASSIVE
INJURY VERSION.  STANDARD FIELD
EQUIPMENT ITEM.

SPECIFICATION:

MODEL: SFAF/SG·MK08-2
SIZE: 2
INTENSITY RANGE: 0 – 500 EmV/AU$^2$
LENGTH OVERALL (CM) _ _ _ _ _ 35
WIDTH OVERALL (CM) _ _ _ _ _ _ 5.6
HEIGHT OVERALL (CM) _ _ _ _ _ 6.95
WEIGHT (GM) _ _ _ _ _ _ _ _ _ 680

Ⓐ HOUSING

Ⓑ REMOVABLE BOTTOM PANEL

Ⓒ ACTIVATING SWITCH – BLACK-OFF
RED-ON (PUSH FORWARD)

Ⓓ INTENSITY CONTROL (DEPRESS TO
INCREASE INTENSITY)

Ⓔ EFFECTIVITY SENSOR

Ⓕ DNA MATCH SYNTHESIZATION UNIT

Ⓖ RAY EMISSION DUCT

Ⓗ RECHARGING CHAMBER

Ⓙ SPECIFICATIONS PLATE

Ⓚ INTENSITY FORCE LIGHT:

0    100   200   300   400   500
OFF              SCALE            FULL

COLORS:

| | | |
|---|---|---|
| ☐ | ANTIMONY | №SF02UC |
| ▨ | GRAY | №SF30UC |
| ▤ | RED | №SF10UC |
| ■ | BLACK | №SF32UC |

0 1 2 3 4 5 6
CENTIMETERS

ROT 90° CCW

TOP PLAN

FRONT ELEVATION

SIDE
PROFILE

# SURGICAL SCALPELS
## STAR FLEET COLLEGE OF MEDICINE STANDARD

MODEL: SFAF/SG-MK10-000
SIZE: 000
CUTTING WIDTH: I AU
INTENSITY RANGE: 0 – 80 EmV/AU²
WEIGHT: 227 GM

PRIME FOCUS

RANGE SCALE LOCK

MODEL: SFAF/SG-MK10-00
SIZE: 00
CUTTING WIDTH: 2 AU
INTENSITY RANGE: 0 – 75 EmV/AU²
WEIGHT: 220 GM

TRIGGER

INTENSITY SCALE

BODY

MODEL: SFAF/SG-MK10-0
SIZE: 0
CUTTING WIDTH: 3 AU
INTENSITY RANGE: 0 – 70 EmV/AU²
WEIGHT: 220 GM

VIEW

CUTTING TIP

ALL:
HOUSING
MATERIAL: RODINIUN
COLOR:
ANTIMONY №SF02UC

SURGEON'S GRIP

0  1  2  3  4
CENTIMETERS

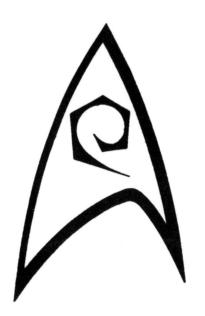

# SUPPORT  SERVICES  SECTION

## SECTION INDEX

| TO. NO: | SUBJECT | CURRENT | REPLACES |
|---|---|---|---|
| 03:00:00 | SUPPORT SERVICES SECTION FLYSHEET | 7305.30 | |
| " " :02 | FOREWORD | * | |
| " " :04 | SUPPORT SERVICES SECTION INDEX | 7504.08 | |
| | | | |
| " :01:00 | COMMUNICATIONS STATION - MAIN BRIDGE | 7408.23 | |
| " " :01 | CONTROLS CONSOLE | 7409.20 | |
| | | | |
| " :02:00 | COMMUNICATOR - TYPE I | 7304.20 | |
| " " :01 | COMMUNICATOR CIRCUITRY | 7304.20 | |
| " " :02 | BRIDGE EAR RECEIVER - MK05 | 7503.07 | |
| " " :03 | B.E.R. CIRCUITRY | * | |
| " " :04 | UNIVERSAL TRANSLATOR - TYPE I | 7503.07 | |
| " " :05 | U/T CIRCUITRY | * | |
| | | | |
| " :05:00 | ENVIRONMENTAL STATION - MAIN BRIDGE | * | |
| " " :01 | CONTROLS CONSOLE | * | |
| | | | |
| " :08:00 | ENGINEERING STATION - MAIN BRIDGE | 7408.23 | |
| " " :01 | CONTROLS CONSOLE | 7409.14 | |
| | | | |
| " " :10 | ENGINEERING SECTION - PRIMARY HULL - CLASS I STARSHIPS | 7312.21 | |
| " " :11 | ENGINEERING SECTION - SECONDARY HULL - MK-IX ONLY | * | |
| | | | |
| " :10:20 | IMPULSE POWER - EXTERNAL PLAN & PROFILE | 7312.21 | |
| " " :21 | IMPULSE POWER - INTERNAL PLAN & PROFILE | CLASSIFIED | |
| | | | |
| " :11:20 | MAIN PROPULSION - EXTERNAL PLAN & PROFILE | 7312.21 | |
| " " :21 | MAIN PROPULSION - INTERNAL PLAN & PROFILE | CLASSIFIED | |
| | | | |
| " :16:30 | TRANSPORTER - STANDARD 6 PERSON - PLAN | 7312.21 | |
| " " :31 | ELEVATIONS | * | |
| | | | |
| " " :50 | TRANSPORTER - EMERGENCY - PLAN | 7312.21 | |
| " " :51 | ELEVATIONS | * | |
| | | | |
| " " :70 | TRANSPORTER - CARGO - PLAN | 7312.21 | |
| " " :71 | ELEVATIONS | * | |
| | | | |
| " :17:00 | HANGAR DECK - PLAN - MK-IX ONLY | 7312.21 | |
| " " :01 | ELEVATION | 7312.21 | |
| | | | |
| | | | |
| | | | |
| | | | |
| | | | |
| | | | |
| | | | |
| " :98:10 | VULCAN LYRETTE | 7503.10 | |
| " " :11 | | * | |
| | | | |
| " " :30 | TRIDIMENSIONAL CHESS | 7503.12 | |
| " " :31 | CHESSMEN | 7503.14 | |
| | | | |

NOTE (*): NO CURRENT PRINT-OUT FROM MASTERCOM DATABANKS/SFHQ

# COMMUNICATIONS
## MAIN BRIDGE STATION - CLASS I STARSHIPS

FRONT ELEVATION

VIEW A-A:

NOTE: CD ~ COMPUTER DATA AND SYSTEMS VISUAL READOUT SCREENS

THIS STATION IS ALSO DUPLICATED ON THE EMERGENCY BRIDGE

ALL EXTRA, AND INTRA-SHIP COMMUNICATIONS ARE HANDLED THROUGH THIS STATION

SEE TO:03:01:01 FOR CONTROLS CONSOLE ARRANGEMENT

OFFICIAL COLORS:

| | | |
|---|---|---|
| | PLATINUM | Nº SF 29 UC |
| | RED | Nº SF 10 UC |
| | GRAY | Nº SF 30 UC |
| | BLACK | Nº SF 32 UC |

0  20  40  60  80
CENTIMETERS

# CONTROLS CONSOLE
VIEW B-B OF TO:03:01:00

REFER ELSEWHERE IN THIS SECTION
FOR DETAILED OPERATIONS PROCED-
URES, AND SYSTEMS FUNCTIONS
SPECIFICATIONS.

REFER TO ENGINEERING SECTION
FOR SYSTEMS SCHEMATICS, WIRING
DIAGRAMS, AND STANDARD MAIN-
TENANCE PROCEDURES.

REFER TO COMMAND SECTION FOR
STAR FLEET SUB-SPACE COMMUNI-
CATIONS CODES (CLASSIFIED).

COMMUNICATIONS SYSTEMS
RECORD DECKS STORAGE
EACH SIDE

ALTERNATE CIRCUITRY AND
EMERGENCY OVERRIDE PANEL

SPECIAL COMMUNICATIONS
FUNCTIONS PATCH-IN PANEL

COMMUNICATIONS INTERCOM

CENTROID OF STATION

SHIP'S INTERNAL COMMUNI-
CATIONS PANEL

CENTROID OF
SEATED BODY

ACTIVE RECORD DECK HOLDER

BRIDGE INTERCOM

SPACE NOISE EMISSIONS
BLANKING CONTROL

EXTERNAL COMMUNICATIONS
PANEL

INTERCOM STATION

OFFICIAL COLORS:
BLUE   No SF 16 UC
BLACK  No SF 32 UC

0  10  20  30  40  50
CENTIMETERS

TYPE I

# COMMUNICATOR
## STANDARD FIELD EQUIPMENT ITEM

SPECIFICATION:
L.O.A.__113.5MM      W.O.A.__63.5MM      H.O.A.__28MM
WEIGHT__200GM        RANGE__12000KM

REMOVABLE BOTTOM

RED (ON) L.E.D.    YELLOW (T) L.E.D.

VENT

TRANSMIT/ RECEIVE SWITCH (SW₁)

ANTENNA

TUNED FERRITE LOOP

CHANNEL SWITCH (SW₂)    BLUE (R) L.E.D.

UPPER BODY SHELL

ANTENNA OPEN

006P ENERGY UNIT (BAT)    SPEAKER/MICROPHONE

COLORS:
| | | |
|---|---|---|
| ☐ GOLD | ANTIMONY | № SF03UC |
| ▨ ANTIMONY | | № SF02UC |
| ▩ BLACK | | № SF32UC |

ATTACH SCREWS (2)    ON/OFF SWITCH (SW)

MAGNATOMIC ADHESION SURFACE

CENTIMETERS
0  1  2  3  4  5

# COMMUNICATOR
## CIRCUITRY DIAGRAM - TYPE I*

ANTENNA – (COVER GRID) – WITH TUNED FERRITE LOOP

SW – ON-OFF SWITCH COVER ACTUATED – TYPE MICRO 1SMI

$SW_1$ – NORMAL RECEIVE (R) PRESS TO TRANSMIT (T) (7 CONTACT)

$SW_2$ – ROTARY 7 CONTACT RF SWITCH

SPKR/MIC – SPEAKER/MICROPHONE – TYPE 32-0214/8Ω/0.1W

| CHANNELS | |
|---|---|
| CH | MHZ |
| OMNI | 27.125 |
| A | 49.91 |
| B | 49.93 |
| C | 49.95 |
| D | 49.97 |
| E | 49.99 |
| F | N.A |

| VALUES | | | | |
|---|---|---|---|---|
| CHANNEL | OMNI | OTHERS | | |
| ENERGY    VDC | 9 | 9 | 15 | 22.5 |
| C1 CAPAC'T'R pF | 100 | | | |
| C2   "   pF | 30 | | | |
| C3   "   μF | .0015 | | | |
| C4   "   μF | .005 | | | |
| C5   "   μF | .02 | | | |
| C6   "   μF | .05 | | | |
| C7   "   pF | 5 | | | |
| C8   "   μF | 1 | | | |
| C9   "   μF | 1 | | | |
| C10   " μF/WV | 30/10 | | | |
| C11   " μF/WV | 30/3 | | | |
| C12   "   μF | .005 | | | |
| C13   " μF/WV | 30/6 | | | |
| C14   " μF/WV | 30/3 | | | |
| C15   "   μF | .02 | | | |
| | | | | |
| D1 ZENER VDC | 1.6 | | | |
| D2   "   VDC | N.R | | | |

| VALUES | | | | |
|---|---|---|---|---|
| CHANNEL | OMNI | OTHERS | | |
| ENERGY    VDC | 9 | 9 | 15 | 22.5 |
| R1 RESISTOR K | 5 | | | |
| R2   "   K | 3.9 | | | |
| R3   "   K | 33 | | | |
| R4   "   Ω | 300 | | | |
| R5   "   Ω | 100 | | | |
| R6   "   K | 5 | | | |
| R7   "   K | 56 | | | |
| R8   "   K | 10 | | | |
| R9   "   Ω | 470 | | | |
| R10   "   Ω | 100 | | | |
| R11   "   K | 3.3 | | | |
| R12   "   Ω | 560 | | | |
| R13   "   Ω | 100 | | | |
| R14   "   Ω | EXP | | | |
| R15   "   Ω | N.R | | | |
| | | | | |
| T1 AUDIO KHZ | 455 | | | |
| T2   "   KHZ | 455 | | | |

*20TH CENTURY TERRAN EARLY DEVELOPMENT

# EAR RECEIVER
## FOR NON-PUBLIC RECEPTION

FOR USE IN CONCENTRATING ON TRANS-
MISSIONS IN ACOUSTICALLY DISTRACTING
SITUATIONS, OR FOR SPECIFIC RECEPTION
OF NON-PUBLIC TRANSMISSIONS

OPERATION IS BY CLOSED LOOP ON ALL
STAR FLEET PRIME COMMUNICATIONS SUB-
SPACE CHANNELS

THE TRANSPARENT HALF-HARD PLASTIC
EAR-PIECE IS CUSTOM MOLDED TO A PRE-
CISE IMPRESSION OF THE USER'S EAR

SPECIFICATION:
        MODEL: SFAF/CC-MK05-0
        SIZE: 0
        LENGTH OVERALL (CM)_ _ _ _ _ _ _6.55
        WIDTH OVERALL (CM)_ _ _ _ _ _ _ _3.15
        MAXIMUM DIAMETER (CM)_ _ _ _ _ _2.6
        WEIGHT (GM)_ _ _ _ _ _ _ _ _ _ _ _57

(A) MOLDED PLASTIC EAR-PIECE
(B) EAR-PIECE RETENTION PLATE
(C) EARPHONE HOUSING
(D) RECEIVER HOUSING
(E) ENERGY CELL HOUSING
(F) HIGH GAIN ANTENNA GRID AND HEAT
    SINK
(G) EAR-PIECE SWIVELS STIFFLY HERE

PLAN          PROFILE

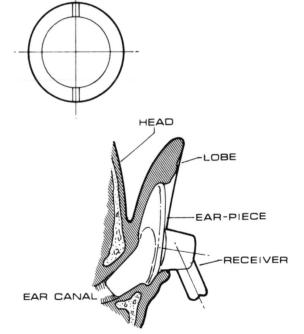

HEAD
LOBE
EAR-PIECE
RECEIVER
EAR CANAL

HORIZONTAL SECTION THROUGH LEFT
EAR AT MID-CANAL LEVEL

COLORS:
☐ ANTIMONY N°SF02UC
▨ BLACK   N°SF32UC

0   1   2   3   4
CENTIMETERS

# UNIVERSAL TRANSLATOR
U.F.P STANDARD

FOR COMMUNICATION BETWEEN UNITED
FEDERATION LANGUAGE FORMS AND WITH
UNKNOWN ALIEN LANGUAGE FORMS IN
THE TREATY EXPLORATION TERRITORY

SPECIFICATION:

    MODEL: SFAF/CC-MK-01

    TYPE: I

    LENGTH OVERALL (CM)_ _ _ _ _ _ 28

    MAXIMUM DIAMETER (CM)_ _ _ _ _ 4.8

    WEIGHT (GM)_ _ _ _ _ _ _ _ _ _ 500

(A) SPEECH CHARACTERISTICS SENSORS

(B) OTHER PARTY SPEAKER/MICROPHONE

(C) DECODING/ENCODING SECTION

(D) COMPUTER FUNCTIONS DISPLAY PANEL

(E) PRIMARY COMPUTER SECTION

(F) OPERATOR'S SPEAKER/MICROPHONE

(G) ACTIVATING SWITCH

(H) DATA STORAGE BANKS SECTION

(J) TRANSPARENT COVER

(K) REAR COVER

(L) HOUSING

45°

OFF

ON

FRONT ELEVATION
ROT 90° CW

SIDE
PROFILE

TOP PLAN

COLORS:

ANTIMONY N°SF02UC

BLACK    N°SF32UC

0  1  2  4  6

CENTIMETERS

# ENGINEERING
## MAIN BRIDGE STATION - CLASS I STARSHIPS

VISUAL INTELLIGENCE DISPLAY

VISUAL INTELLIGENCE DISPLAY

CD  CD  CD  CD      CD  CD  CD  CD

BRIDGE VENTILATION

OPERATOR'S CHAIR

FRONT ELEVATION

VIEW A-A:

110° SCAN

CIRCULAR ARC BACK

50% TILE EYE POINT

90° SCAN

CONTROLS CONSOLE

RAILING

MAIN BRIDGE DECK

NOTE:  CD—COMPUTER DATA AND SYSTEMS VISUAL READOUT SCREENS

THIS IS A SLAVE STATION CAPABLE OF HANDLING THE SHIP'S IMPORTANT ENGINEERING FUNCTIONS. ALL PRIMARY CONTROL IS LOCATED IN THE ENGINEERING DIVISION

SEE TO:03:08:01 FOR CONTROLS CONSOLE ARRANGEMENT

OFFICIAL COLORS:

| | | |
|---|---|---|
| | PLATINUM | № SF 29 UC |
| | RED | № SF 10 UC |
| | GRAY | № SF 30 UC |
| | BLACK | № SF 32 UC |

0  20  40  60  80
CENTIMETERS

# CONTROLS CONSOLE
VIEW B-B OF TO:03:08:00

REFER ELSEWHERE IN THIS SECTION
FOR DETAILED OPERATIONS PROCED-
URES, AND SYSTEMS FUNCTIONS
SPECIFICATIONS.

REFER ELSEWHERE IN THIS SECTION
FOR SYSTEM SCHEMATICS, WIRING
DIAGRAMS, AND STANDARD MAIN-
TENANCE PROCEDURES.

ENGINEERING SYSTEMS
RECORD DECKS STORAGE

SHIP'S HIGH-ENERGY SYSTEMS
SLAVE CONTROL PANEL

MALFUNCTION INDICATORS

ENGINEERING INTERCOM

ENGINEERING FUNCTIONS
PATCH-IN PANEL

CENTROID OF STATION

CENTROID OF
SEATED BODY

IMPULSE POWER UNITS
SLAVE CONTROL PANEL

CRITICAL REGIME INDICATOR

ACTIVE RECORD DECKS HOLDER

MAIN PROPULSION UNITS
SLAVE CONTROL PANEL

INTERCOM STATION

TYPE SP-HCA/RVS-I SCANNER

OFFICIAL COLORS:
BLUE  N°SF16UC
BLACK N°SF32UC

0 10 20 30 40 50
CENTIMETERS

# ENGINEERING SECTION
## PRIMARY HULL - CLASS I STARSHIPS

STBD
MAIN CORRIDOR P/S

HEAT EXCHANGER P/S

SUMP TANK TOP P/S

EXTERNAL HULL SHELL

ENGINEERING COMPUTER ROOM

MAIN CORRIDOR P/S

GANGWAY P/S

RAILING P/S

ENERGY CONVERTER P/S

CORRIDOR P/S

MAIN FUNCTIONS TRANSFER PANEL

(HI-BAY)          RAILING

REMOTE SCANNERS MONITORING ROOM

TWIN

ACCESS DOOR TO CARGO HOLDS P/S

MAIN CONTROLS CONSOLES

(A) ACCESS DOOR TO ELEVATOR MAINTENANCE SHOP P/S

IMPULSE

TURBO-ELEVATOR CAR

(B) COMPUTER SYSTEMS MONITORING BOARD

(C) STAND-BY POWER UNIT

(D) IMPULSE SYNCROTRON UNIT

-HI-BAY-

POWER

TOOL CRIB & PARTS SHOP

DOUBLE SECURITY DOOR-TYP

(E) TERTIARY STANDARDS ROOM

(HI-BAY)

CHIEF ENGINEER'S OFFICE

UNITS (4)

GANGWAY

15 KG/CM² OVER-PRESSURE CONST.

SMALL PARTS SHOP

(F) CORRIDOR

SUMP TANK P/S

TOILET P/S

DECK 7 PLAN

PORT          DECK 6 PLAN

TOILET

PRECISION INSTRUMENT SHOP

0   2   4   6   8
METERS

# IMPULSE POWER UNIT
## CLASS I STARSHIPS - EXTERNAL ARRANGEMENT

- (A) TWIN UNIT HOUSING
- (B) FIELD FLUX DIP CONSTRICTION
- (C) MAGNATOMIC FLUX CIRCULATION TUBES (12)
- (D) FUEL HOPPER FEED CHUTE
- (E) FLUX RECIRCULATION TUBES TO HEAT EXCHANGERS (5)
- (F) FIRING CHAMBER (2)

TOP PLAN

SPECIFICATIONS:

LENGTH OVERALL (M) _ _ _ _ _ _ 5.2
WIDTH OVERALL (M) _ _ _ _ _ _ _ 4.5
HEIGHT OVERALL (M) _ _ _ _ _ _ 2.8
WEIGHT - D.W.T (M.T) _ _ _ _ _ _ 2800
MODEL: IP186E/2-IR

OPERATION IS BASED ON SUBATOMIC
UNIFIED ENERGY IMPULSE POSTULATE

POWER IS REVERSIBLE BY PROPER CONTROL
OF THE EXTERNAL VENT SHIELDS

PORT PROFILE

ELEVATIONS

FRONT                              REAR

0        1        2        3
METERS

# MAIN PROPULSION
## CLASS I STARSHIPS - EXTERNAL ARRANGEMENT

(A) SPACE ENERGY/MATTER SINK (ACQUISITION)

(B) SPACE ENERGY FIELD SENSOR (3)

(C) MAGNATOMIC FLUX CONSTRICTION – FIRST STAGE

(D) INLET FLOW SENSOR

(E) CONTROL REACTOR LOOP (PRIMARY POWER STAGE)

(F) OUTLET FLOW SENSOR

(G) POWER STAGE MAGNATOMIC FLUX CHILLER (3)

(H) MAIN ENERGY STAGE MAGNATOMIC FLUX CHILLER (5)

(J) MAIN PROPULSION HOUSING (NACELLE - AND DEFLECTOR SHIELD)

(K) FINAL STAGE INTERCOOLERS P/S

(L) FINAL STAGE MAGNATOMIC FLUX CHILLERS P/S

(N) SPACE ENERGY/MATTER MATTRIX RESTORATION COWL

(O) SPACE ENERGY/MATTER SOURCE (FIELD RESTORATION)

SUPPORT PYLON LOCATIONS:

(P) MK-X DREADNOUGHT NO.'S I AND 3

(R) MK-X DREADNOUGHT NO. 2

(S) MK-IX HEAVY CRUISER NO.'S I AND 2

(T) MK-VIII DESTROYER NO. I
MK-VII SCOUT NO. I

(U) MK-VI TRANSPORT/TUG NO.'S I & 2

NOTE: UNIT (V) IS ROTATED 90° TO BOTTOM ₵ ON MK-VIII AND MK-VII MODELS

SPECIFICATIONS:
    LENGTH OVERALL: (M) _ _ _ _ 153.619
    MAX. DIAMETER: (M) _ _ _ _ _ _ _ 17.3
    WEIGHT –D.W.T: (M.T.) _ _ _ _ _ 31,000
    MODEL: SW40/5-3KT

OPERATION IS BASED ON UNIFIED FIELD SPACE ENERGY/MATTER MATTRIX WARP POSTULATE

THE SYSTEM IS REVERSIBLE WITH MODERATE POWER CAPABILITY AND MINIMUM SPACE E/M MATTRIX DEGRADATION

STARBOARD OR INBOARD SIDE PROFILE

ROT 90° CW

45°

ROT 90° CCW

PORT OR OUTBOARD SIDE PROFILE

₵

120°

45°

ROT 90° CCW

0    10    20    30
METERS

# TRANSPORTER
## STANDARD 6 PERSON - PRIMARY HULL - CLASS I STARSHIPS

DECK 7 PLAN

PROTECTIVE BARRIER

TRANSPORTER NO. 1

TURBO-ELEVATOR STATION

T/E SHAFT

TRANSPORT MACHINERY ROOM

T/E CAR

CONTROLS CONSOLE

COMPUTER

SHIP'S SERVICE

POCKET DOORS

PORT SIDE

ATHWARTSHIP ℄

MEDICAL SECTION LOBBY

ENERGY DISCHARGE BANK

STEPS UP

MAIN CORRIDOR

HAZARD GEAR AND OTHER ARTICLE STOWAGE

COMPUTER FUNCTIONS MONITOR

TRANSPORT UNIT (6)

TRANSPORTER NO. 3

TRANSPORTERS NO!S 2 AND 4 ON STARBOARD SIDE DIRECTLY OPPOSITE

0 1 2 3 4 5
METERS

# TRANSPORTER
## EMERGENCY - PRIMARY HULL - CLASS I STARSHIPS

DECK 8 PLAN

MAXIMUM CAPACITY - 22 PERSONS

TRANSPORT MACHINERY UNDER

POCKET DOORS - TYP

TRANSPORT UNIT (22)

STEPS

UP

FWD

℄ SHIP

TRANSPORTER NO. 7

CONTROLS CONSOLE

COMPUTER FUNCTIONS MONITOR

TRANSPORTER NO. 7 (FWD) SHOWN.
NO. 5 (PORT SIDE - REAR QUARTER)
SAME PLAN.  NO. 6 (STBD SIDE -
REAR QUARTER) REVERSE PLAN.

0        1        2        3        4
METERS

# TRANSPORTER
## CARGO - PRIMARY HULL - CLASS I STARSHIPS

DECK 10 PLAN

DOORS

CAPACITY (BULK SIZE IN METERS)
UP TO: 2.8L x 2.5W x 2.0H
OR: 3.45L x 1.0W x 2.0H

COMPUTER FUNCTIONS MONITOR

TRANSPORTER NO. 8

CARGO

HANDLING

FLOOR

¢ SHIP

AFT

TRANSPORT UNIT
(96 SEGMENTS)

CONTROLS CONSOLE

DOORS

0   1   2   3
METERS

# HANGAR DECK
## MK-IX MODEL ONLY - CLASS I STARSHIPS

DECK 19 PLAN

AIR SUPPLY DUCT-P/S

SUPPORT PYLON FWD.
STRUCTURAL BLHD.-P/S

POCKET DOORS TO
CORRIDOR-P/S

FLUSH HATCH-GANGWAY
TO DECK 20 SHOPS

POCKET DOORS TO
ELEVATOR LOBBY

SPACE STORAGE POCKET
P/S

SUPPORT PYLON AFT
STRUCTURAL BLHD-P/S

ELEVATOR TO DECK 20
MAINTENANCE SHOPS

TURNTABLE IN ELEV.

PIPING & WIRING TRUNK
P/S

OBSERVATION GALLERY
OVER & AROUND

SCALING LADDERS-F/A
P/S

POCKET TO OPERATIONS
TOWER-P/S

SHUTTLECRAFT RESERVE
FUEL STORAGE-P/S

DECK OPERATIONS CONT.
TOWER OVER-P/S

FLUSH CARGOHOLD
HATCH-P/S

CLAMSHELL HANGAR
DOORS (6 SEGMENT)

SPOT LANDING TARGET
PAINTED ON DECK

STERN FANTAIL

COLORS:
TAUPE    N°SF28UC
YELLOW  N°SF12UC
RED       N°SF09UC

0  2  4  6  8  10
METERS

# HANGAR DECK
## PRINCIPAL ELEVATION - MK-IX MODEL ONLY

PORT SIDE

SUPPORT PYLON FWD
STRUCTURAL BLHD

OBSERVATION GALLERY

LANDING TRACTOR
BEAM ROOM

SUPPORT PYLON AFT
STRUCTURAL BLHD

TRACTOR BEAM

HANGAR SHELL

AIR INLET DUCT - P/S

EXTERIOR HULL SHELL

LANDING FLOODLIGHT - P/S

DECK OPERATIONS
CONTROL TOWER - P/S

HOMING BEACON AND
NAVIGATIONAL ARRAY

COSMIC RAY SHIELD

CLAMSHELL HANGAR DOORS

ELEVATOR LOBBY

STORAGE POCKET
HANGAR DECK

WORKBENCHES

SHUTTLECRAFT
MAINTENANCE
SHOPS

ELEVATOR AND
TURNTABLE

DECK 20

POCKET TO SCALING
LADDERS

STORAGE SPACE

SHUTTLECRAFT
RESERVE FUEL
STORAGE - P/S

DECK 19

CARGOHOLDS - P/S

FANTAIL COVE

HANGAR DOORS OPERATING
MACHINERY FLAT

0   2   4   6   8   10
METERS

# VULCAN LYRETTE
## ORCHESTRAL MODEL MUSICAL INSTRUMENT

AN UNUSUALLY HARMONIOUS AND MELODIC ACCOMPANIMENT OR SOLO INSTRUMENT WHOSE ORIGIN IS LOST IN VULCAN ANTIQUITY. IT COMBINES THE TONAL QUALITIES OF A HARP, LUTE, SITAR, AND TO SOME EXTENT, VIOLIN.

THE MOST FAMOUS MODELS WERE MADE BY SARPK SOME 5 VULCAN CENTURIES AGO OF WHICH, SOME 300 ARE KNOWN TO STILL BE IN EXISTENCE. OTHER FAMOUS MODELS WERE MADE BY SAJEK OF VULCAN AND SEPAR OF TRILAN.

THE TONAL PATTERN IS MODAL DIA-TONIC RATHER THAN CHROMATIC AND REQUIRES A HIGH DEGREE OF SKILL TO PERFORM IN THIS REGISTRATION.

WHILE A SKILLED PERFORMER MANIPULATES THE STRINGS WITH THE FINGERS OF THE RIGHT HAND, A PLECTRUM MAY ALSO BE USED.

PITCH RANGE:
LOWEST — 60 CPS
HIGHEST — 3180 CPS

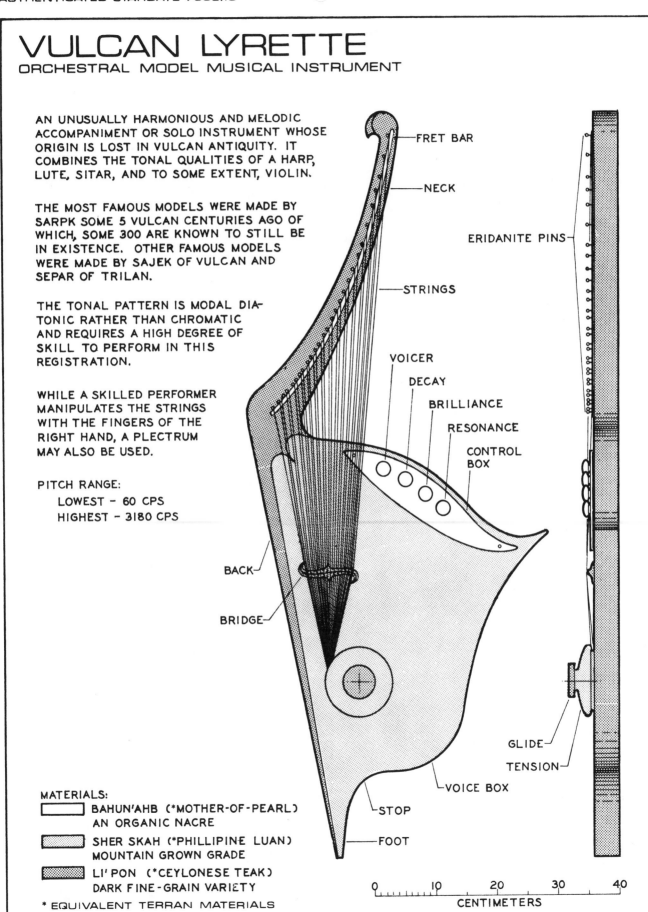

FRET BAR
NECK
ERIDANITE PINS
STRINGS
VOICER
DECAY
BRILLIANCE
RESONANCE
CONTROL BOX
BACK
BRIDGE
GLIDE
TENSION
VOICE BOX
STOP
FOOT

MATERIALS:
BAHUN'AHB (*MOTHER-OF-PEARL) AN ORGANIC NACRE
SHER SKAH (*PHILLIPINE LUAN) MOUNTAIN GROWN GRADE
LI'PON (*CEYLONESE TEAK) DARK FINE-GRAIN VARIETY

* EQUIVALENT TERRAN MATERIALS

0    10    20    30    40
CENTIMETERS

# TRIDIMENSIONAL CHESS
## REGULATION TOURNAMENT BOARD

THIS IS THE MOST
COMPLEX FORM OF THE
ANCIENT GAME OF
CHESS YET DEVISED.
IT IS NORMALLY STUDIED
AND ATTEMPTED ONLY
BY PERSONS WITH
MASTER'S SKILLS IN
THE ORDINARY FORM
OF THE GAME.

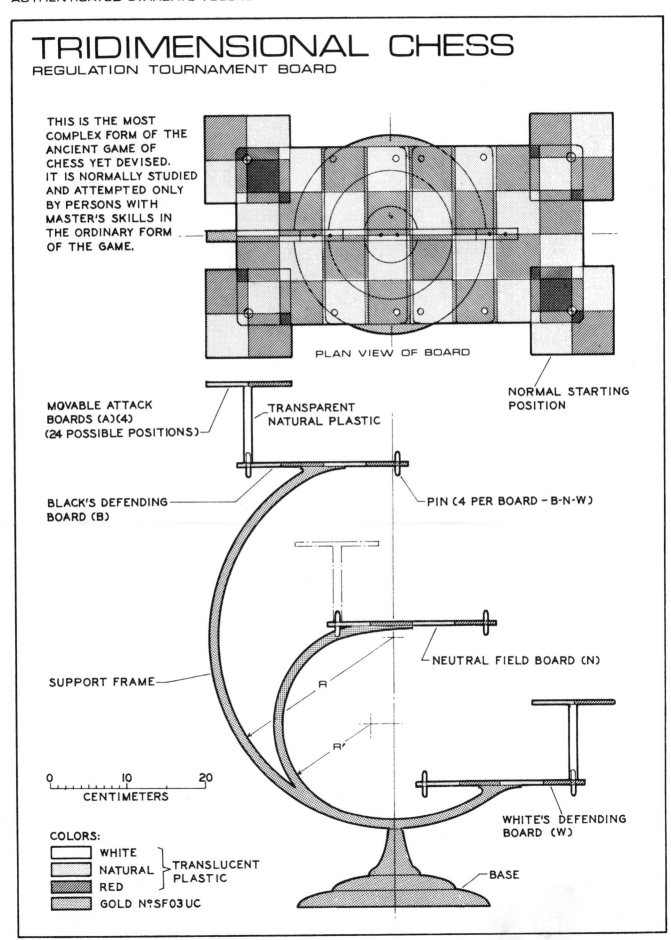

PLAN VIEW OF BOARD

NORMAL STARTING
POSITION

MOVABLE ATTACK
BOARDS (A)(4)
(24 POSSIBLE POSITIONS)

TRANSPARENT
NATURAL PLASTIC

BLACK'S DEFENDING
BOARD (B)

PIN (4 PER BOARD — B-N-W)

NEUTRAL FIELD BOARD (N)

SUPPORT FRAME

R

R'

WHITE'S DEFENDING
BOARD (W)

0    10    20
CENTIMETERS

BASE

COLORS:
- WHITE ⎱
- NATURAL ⎰ TRANSLUCENT PLASTIC
- RED
- GOLD Nº SF03 UC

# TRIDIMENSIONAL CHESS
## REGULATION TOURNAMENT PLAYING PIECES

THE IDENTIFICATION OF EACH PIECE
GIVES ITS NAME – POINT VALUE – AND
QUANTITY. A STARTING SIDE, WHITE OR
BLACK, IS 16 PIECES AND 39 POINTS

KING 0   QUEEN 9   BISHOP 3 (2)   KNIGHT 3 (2)   ROOK 5 (2)   PAWN 1 (8)

THE BLACK SET OF CHESSMEN IS IDENTICAL
TO THE WHITE SET EXCEPT FOR ITS COLOR

THE SIZE, SHAPE, AND VISUAL APPEARANCE
OF EACH PIECE IS OF PRIME IMPORTANCE TO
MENTAL RECOGNITION OF THE POWER
PATTERN ON THE BOARD AT ANY POINT IN
THE PLAY

REFER TO THE GENERAL BIBLIOGRAPHY
SECTION FOR TEXTS ON THE FUNDAMENT-
ALS OF TRIDIMENSIONAL CHESS

EACH PIECE MOVES EXACTLY THE SAME AS
IN CONVENTIONAL CHESS EXCEPT THAT
SUCH MOVES HAVE TRIDIMENSIONAL FREE-
DOM TO THE EXTENT OF AVAILABLE CON-
SECUTIVE SQUARES

16 OF THE 64 SQUARES ARE MOVABLE IN
4 GROUPS OF 4 SQUARES EACH. THEY MAY
BE MOVE TO ONE ADJACENT PIN POSITION
AT A TIME PROVIDED THEY ARE EITHER
VACANT OR OCCUPIED BY ONLY ONE OF
THE PLAYER'S PAWNS, AND SUCH ACTION
CONSTITUTES A MOVE IN REGULAR TURN.
AN OCCUPIED ATTACK BOARD CANNOT BE
MOVED TO AN INVERTED PIN POSITION

0 1 2 3 4 5 6
CENTIMETERS

STARTING ARRANGEMENT:

BLACK

WHITE

# MISCELANEOUS SECTION

# STAR FLEET COMMAND
## STAR FLEET HEADQUARTERS
# UNITED FEDERATION OF PLANETS

FRANZ JOSEPH
UNITED FEDERATION REPRESENTATIVE                    STARDATE 7504

## APPENDIX  A

### TO ALL CIVILIAN AUXILIARIES OF SFAF,
### UNITED NATIONS/EARTH/SOL SYSTEM

THE TECHNICAL ORDERS COMPRISING THIS SECTION WERE NOT INCLUDED IN

THE UNORTHODOX TRANSMISSION OF STARDATE 3113.   UNTIL SUCH TIME AS

THESE DATA CAN BE MADE AVAILABLE, WE SUGGEST YOU CONSIDER USING

THIS SECTION TO FILE MISCELANEOUS INFORMATION YOU HAVE COLLECTED

IN THE GENERAL SUBJECT AREAS OF THE TECHNICAL MANUAL

SUBJECT

STARDATE

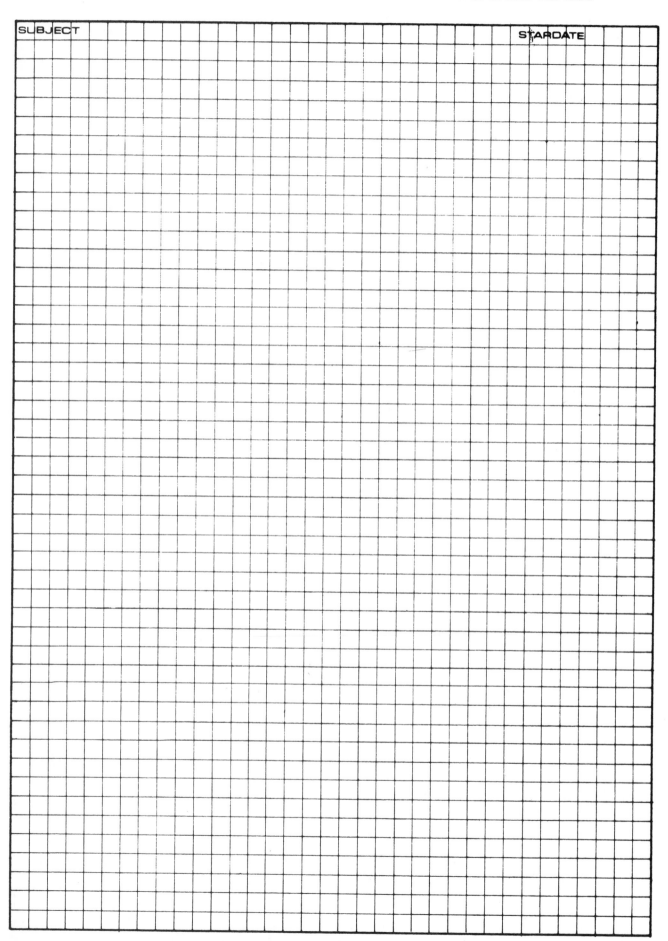

CADET _____

DIVISION _____

TM:379260-

# THE STAR FLEET ACADEMY
FORM 04:01:01 THE CADET SCHOOL

SUBJECT

STARDATE

SUBJECT                                                                    STARDATE

CADET_____

DIVISION_____

TM:379260-

# THE STAR FLEET ACADEMY

FORM 04:01:01 THE CADET SCHOOL

SUBJECT

STARDATE

| SUBJECT | | | | | | | | | | | | | | | | | | | | | STARDATE | | | |

# THE STAR FLEET ACADEMY

FORM 04:01:01 THE CADET SCHOOL

CADET_____

DIVISION_____

SUBJECT

STARDATE

THE STAR FLEET ACADEMY

TM:379260

FORM 04:01:01 THE CADET SCHOOL